MARCOS BETRAYAL

THE SECRETS OF THE ORB

MJ ANAND

ISBN 979-8-88959-607-3

This trilogy is dedicated to the special forces personnel working across Asia.

CHARACTER TREE

RAW	Rajnish Gogoi, Head of RAW Operations	Amjad, Special Secretary, Defense Attache
Border Intelligence	Sunaina Singh, Chief of Border Intelligence	Major general Akash, Field Operative
Marcos	Lt General Bikram Restage, Head of MARCOS	Abhimanyu Singh, Field Operative
Intelligence Bureau	Prem Golwaonkar, Director General, IB	Major General Arup, Head, Eastern Sector, IB
The Tunnel	Arnab Roy, Head of Tunnel	Uday Kumar, ISRO Chief

CONTENTS

PREFACE

The first real espionage novel I read was Robert Ludlum's *Bourne Identity* almost two decades ago. In one book series, Jason Bourne enriched the imagination of audiences more than the many Bond movies had managed in the last several decades, as they say no movie can beat a good book. No wonder when a close movie adaption of the *Bourne* book series was launched in 2002 James Bond had to go home. When it's your day, you just can't die another day. A misogynist, imperialist, queen-obsessed, gun-wielding spy was now a thing of the past. To reinvent James Bond, even the movies resurrected the first novel, *Casino Royale*, published in 1953. Again, as they say, no movie can beat a good book. Ian Flemings's words were always more meaningful than the movies were ever, and *Casino Royale* was possibly the best of the lot. *Bourne* changed the discourse, but it was still a white man's world. It still is.

When you are born in India, in Asia, you are born to survive. To survive the famines that could have been avoided, the epidemics that could have been stopped, and the wars that never resolved any dispute. Unlike Europe, wars have a long life in Asia. World War I ended in five years, and World War II ended in six years, but the Asians typically just get started in six years. Take the Koreans for example. The North and South have been at loggerheads with each other since first half of nineteenth century, but the core issue is still unresolved. Similarly, India and Pakistan have fought four wars since independence, but the core issue is still unresolved. That is seventy long years of fighting in each case. Another example is the Vietnam War that lasted twenty years of active fighting. In those twenty years, the American military went from being the World War heroes to a shadow of itself when it evacuated its last personnel from Saigon in 1975.

Despite its firepower, the superpower had been humbled in the streets of modern-day Ho Chi Minh and the flat flood plains of the Mekong Delta. The fall of Saigon changed the US military's legacy. Meanwhile, the American public went from being a great supporter of the war in 1955 to being a great supporter of the withdrawal. Whether it was an issue of human rights or not, the Vietnamese had successfully won the battle of perceptions as well. Let's not forget this was during a time when the concept of psychological warfare to influence enemies population in your favor did not exist. The Vietnamese knew none of it; they just returned to basic and held their ground. When it became difficult to hold the ground, they just went underground—quite literally in the Cu Chi tunnels. The American troops couldn't survive a week in those tunnels. The Vietnamese survived twenty years. Their tenacity broke the back of the American military and public alike. That's what a war of attrition can do. I wouldn't even get started on what Afghanistan did to the two superpowers. But why am I outlining these events when this book talks about none of those?

Ironically, all my favorite characters are non-Asian. Ludlum's Bourne, Flemings's Bond, Le Carre's Smiley, Forsyth's Jackal, or even Greene's Wormold is a white man out to save the whole world. Even the plots avoid Asia almost systematically. Greene's Wormold and Flemings's Bond go to Cuba, and that's perhaps the farthest they manage from the shores of Europe. It's not their mistake, for the narratives have been focused on the World Wars and the Cold War for far too long. But, even by population odds, one of these five all-time favorite characters could have been an Asian.

These observations, alongside my experiences, led me to write this series. A spy in Asia is not just supposed to track a nuke or build on a queen's aura, but he is meant to survive each day and every hour of an attritional war that could last decades. Most don't survive, but some do, and that's why the nations still survive.

It was a typical north Indian cold winter morning on 13 December 2001. We hadn't even finished the first hour in school when we heard the news of the attack on the Indian Parliament. We were in a cantonment near the

India-Pakistan border, and an eerie silence had overtaken the campus. By the time the students left school, MiGs were buzzing through the skies every hour or so. I lived on one end of the town with nothing but thirty miles of sand separating us from the border. Within two days, an armored tank battalion had taken over the horizons across the sand. Things escalated quickly, and within a week, MiGs had completely overtaken the skies, tanks were moving around my back yard, and military trucks were all one could find in this small town of barely a lakh population. I would witness the troika every day on my trip to school. We knew the final curtain had been drawn when my father got the steel locket that had his blood type, service number, and religion embossed. It was to ensure they knew how to deal with him if he got injured or died. The families were ordered to move out soon as the war trumpet was blown. It never did. Having seen the preparations, I wondered why?

This was my first-hand experience of what a war looked like from close quarters. I started reading up and taking interest in stories all around me. Most of them were from the Cold War era, but a few from Asia also intrigued me. One such story was the story of Ajit Doval, the Indian bureaucrat who rose through the ranks in field. He spent seven years in Pakistan and even posed as a Pakistani spy to negotiate with the Khalistani terrorists in Golden Temple.

On the global stage, the Cox report of 1999 put forth the activities of the Chinese authorities in public glare. The Chinese sabotaged every thermonuclear device in the US arsenal by collecting many small pieces of information through the many Chinese students and scholars. The Americans were not used to such well-orchestrated mass sabotage plans where it was just too difficult to build evidence against any individual suspect. The new Asian age had arrived, and the Americans were frustrated to publicly accept their own mistakes. In 2016, the US Justice Department finally charged China Nuclear General Power Group with stealing nuclear secrets from the United States. Another very interesting espionage story in Asia unfolded when the CIA lost eighteen to twenty assets in China in a span of two years between 2010 to 2012. While the *New York Times* did a lengthy expose on it, no one from CIA or anyone in China ever commented on it. The number of assets lost in China rivaled those lost during the betrayal of Aldrich Ames and Robert Hansenn who divulged classified information to Moscow for years. I haven't even touched the Japanese and the West Asian desert kingdoms.

Many such interesting stories, along with my childhood experience of living close with the military men, no doubt, inspired me to write this marine trilogy. Then came my travels through Asia and my eyes just opened up to the vast possibility of stories that can be built around the brave men and women who traverse through these beautiful landscapes. From the Great Himalayas to the vast Gobi desert, from the white sand beaches of Korea to the brown sand trenches of Iraq, Asia has a lot to offer and a lot to defend. This is the story of its defenders, and this book is the second of six volumes in the *Marcos* trilogy.

...START...
THE SECRETS OF THE ORB

CHAPTER 13

THE URGE

RAW Safehouse, New Delhi

RAW's Delhi hideout was far from the headquarters uptown, which was often under the sharp eyes of enemies scanning the movements. It was a general espionage objective to track anyone who enters or leaves the intelligence headquarters of enemy nations. Sometimes, they tracked it even for friendly nations, be it the Americans, Pakistanis, Chinese, or even the Russians. Everyone had assets in place to game the law enforcement agencies of the land and prey on each other's intelligence headquarters. A cat and mouse game ensued almost always.

Amjad had reached the hideout early morning. Abhimanyu had barely got a full night's sleep but managed to turn up in his pajama and tee. Amjad had sounded unusually rushed on the call earlier. He expected Amjad to be relieved now. Perhaps he was here for a firsthand debrief before the formalities of the headquarter took over later in the day.

Abhimanyu entered the hallway with his eyes still red. 'There was no need to come all the way here.'

Amjad rushed him back to his room and closed the door.

'Well, I had to. Of all the people I can think of, only you would know about it more than me.' Amjad threw a red file across the table toward Abhimanyu.

He was taken aback by Amjad's anxiety. The file was a regular autopsy report of Major General Akash's death.

'Go to page eleven.'

Abhimanyu shuffled through the pages titled, Prime Suspect. It had the fingerprints, shoe prints, and the DNA report of the prime suspect in Major General Akash's death.

'It matches this report.' Amjad threw another file.

Abhimanyu didn't need to go beyond the first page. The file had an all-too-familiar face, that of Mohamad Ali, alias Pasha. He could make sense of Amjad's hostility now. Amjad probably knew about Abhimanyu's meeting with Pasha, but such hostility was still baffling. 'So, why are you telling me?' He tried to lead Amjad.

'Last time we spoke about it, you didn't tell me the whole story.'

Abhimanyu looked the other way.

'Do you know him?'

'I can't recall.'

Amjad was furious at Abhimanyu's reply, for he indeed had more evidence to push him to a corner. 'This may help you to recall.' Amjad opened a few photographs.

Someone had clicked Abhimanyu with Pasha just after he had located Mohamad Ali, just before he had to chase him down the narrow lanes of Srinagar.

'Would it make any difference if I had known him?'

'It would make all the difference. He was responsible for Akash's death. Intelligence Bureau had a notice on him, but they couldn't locate him. Guess how they found him.'

'How?'

'They found him because they had a track on you when you disappeared conveniently in Kashmir. Nobody escapes their eyes in Kashmir.' Amjad was a little confused, for Abhimanyu still did not show an expression of guilt. 'You knew the person they couldn't find for months despite having his biometric details from the death site. He almost didn't exist, if not for his involvement in Akash's death.'

'Did you have a tag on me everywhere I went?'

'You went on a holiday during a mission. What are we supposed to do?'

Head in his hands, Abhimanyu sat on his chair.

'In fact, it was I who asked IB to tag you. They went one step further and verified the people you met in Kashmir.'

Abhimanyu raised his head. He had heard enough. It was disaster. Pasha's identity had been exposed. 'That mission was on a break for a reason.'

'It was a break that landed you in the hotbed of insurgency in Kashmir with Pasha who killed Akash. So, tell me your break had a better reason.'

Abhimanyu took a deep breath to think. Amjad, and now IB, had a tag on him. So could he really trust Amjad? He had led IB to him, to Pasha. Pasha had successfully hidden from the unknown enemies for so long but no longer. Abhimanyu still didn't know the mole's identity, and Pasha was his only hope to get to the mole—his best bet to screen all Akash's communications, decrypt it and get the leads to the mole.

'If it helps, he's been killed.' Amjad threw the information nonchalantly to gauge Abhimanyu's reaction.

Abhimanyu was stunned. In shock, he barely managed a stone face. Another line of lead had disappeared. He felt angry and guilty for having led the forces to Pasha. Major General Akash's missions were again a black box. Khalid was the mastermind, but he was a known enemy. Who was the unknown enemy? The mole had impregnated himself so well he could clear out libraries and flawlessly use the Indian intelligence setup against the Indians. It was time to put up his guard, even with Amjad. He needed another play now—a play on Amjad to start with. 'Why did you kill him?'

Amjad was surprised to see a new inquisitive Abhimanyu. The spy in Abhimanyu had resurfaced. The guilt had disappeared. He was in no mood for any nonsense. 'Do you still need to ask? He killed Major General Akash. We killed him.'

'How do you know he was the killer?'

'Listen, kid. I'm not here to answer your questions. The two files you have in front of you explain everything you need to know. IB had identified him as the murderer, and his biometrics matched with what we had collected from the murder site. All the biometrics.'

'So, by *we*, you mean someone in IB had identified him as the murderer.'

Amjad didn't take time to understand what he meant.

'I need to know who is that someone. Who fed you the information?'

'For your comfort, I can say it has been verified by the best, and it can't be wrong.'

Abhimanyu read between the lines. It went even above Amjad, who was being led on not only by the leads but also by command. Someone senior in IB was involved or even someone junior in a staff role in an important office, able to feed this information to the seniors. He couldn't be sure, and he couldn't do much now, for he had been tagged already.

Abhimanyu did a quick calculation in his mind. Pasha was gone; he needed a new lead. He couldn't get it on his own. So, this conversation was the only thing he could play. Amjad had more access to the Indian intelligence systems than Abhimanyu, and the mole had already played Amjad. Abhimanyu had to track the trail back to, hopefully, find a lead to the mole. The only blessing in disguise was that in getting Pasha killed, the mole had exposed his play. He had proven his existence in the IB. Now, Abhimanyu had to capture Amjad's curiosity without playing into his hands. 'I can prove your lead was wrong.'

'Go on. Prove it.'

'A few days ago, someone dropped a mobile phone into my pocket in the busy streets of Delhi. It rang, and when I connected, it was Pasha on the other end. He asked me to come to Kashmir, alone.'

Amjad was intrigued.

'Alone, so he could share some information. When I met him, he explained everything that had happened on that fateful night.'

Amjad's face wrinkled in confusion.

'Major General Akash had called him to hand over some information marked highly critical by Akash himself. He was there on time, but Akash was no longer alive.'

'Why didn't you tell me any of this the last time I confronted you?'

'Would you expose your asset so easily? I had to save his identity. From everyone. Even you.'

Amjad was pensive; Abhimanyu sensed the discomfort. The thought of having killed the wrong lead or an important lead, one's own lead, would be very perturbing to any officer—at least to the ones whose hearts were in right place. But Amjad was not quick to jump the gun. 'You didn't do a good job at that, surely. You need to give me something concrete to believe you.'

Abhimanyu stood and spoke in low voice. 'Pasha gave me the Kulnagar coordinates. Khalid has been captured because of Pasha.'

Pasha's information had proven to be credible. Major General Akash could have shared such information only with a close confidant. Amjad realized he had screwed up, for an ordinary terrorist would never know the future plans of someone like Khalid. In disbelief, he pushed his thoughts further. If Pasha was an assassin sent just to kill Major General Akash, he would mostly be a sleeper resource—someone who laid low, far from the top leadership's communication lines, a contracted third-party resource or someone junior enough in the hierarchy sent to close the last mile of an operation.

It had to be someone with Major General Akash's skillsets who could filter Khalid's details from the Pakistani system, and, if Major General Akash had shared these co-ordinates with anyone, he was his trusted aide—a friend of India, not foe.

But the IB couldn't have gone so wrong either. Amjad's mind was befuddled. He had too many unanswered questions. He needed time to get those answered. Amjad sat by the sofa to collect himself. 'If what you say is true, it's devastating. We have been compromised.'

Finally, Abhimanyu thought he had Amjad's ears. He leaned forward. 'You need to tell me who forwarded you the information.'

Amjad regained his thoughts and faced him. 'As much as I wish to now, I can't. But I promise you, I'll get to the bottom of this and find the truth.'

Amjad had stonewalled him. Abhimanyu was desperate to have a lead, but he had no other option but to wait. 'Do it before it's too late.'

The shock for Amjad was too much, and the implications of his actions were too many. Amjad nodded and left quickly without much to say.

Abhimanyu watched him leave the compound from the window. Things were moving too fast, and he could feel an impending doom. He stared at the sky and broke down, for he had led the intelligence teams to Pasha and another life's worth was balanced against his own life now.

IB Headquarters, New Delhi

It was January twelfth, and the morning office hours had just started. MARCOS arrived at the fifth floor of the Delhi headquarters via a basement lift. Members of covert communications teams who facilitated class-four missions worked from this floor. They were the ones who fed Sonia with all the right feeds in the cross-border operation. This was also the floor from where Amjad and his team of class-four officers operated. The roads of bureaucracy that led to the Defense Ministry in south block started here. In the larger context, this was the only team who knew the details of the impending nuclear strike apart from the designated senior officials—the Prime Minister of India, National Security Advisor, heads of IB, Raw, and later on, Border Intelligence.

The mission was a success. The Indians didn't need to abandon their assets. For all the investments made in the MARCOS, the establishment wouldn't have thought twice. Now that it had gone well, NSA was more than happy to apprise the prime minister of it.

Abhimanyu looked around. The security firewall was outside this room. Perhaps the mole was watching him right now. Then he recalled the protocols. No one here would have known the mission details till the mission was over. They operated blind till the mission was accomplished successfully. Perhaps that's why MARCOS could still pull it off. They were ahead all the time.

Definitely not everywhere. The cyber cell in the Tunnel hadn't cracked the hard disk yet. Thankfully, the RAW had Khalid now—the key to all those secrets hidden in that hard disk. Hopefully, it will halt the strike. Abhimanyu saw the cyber team, who were called in to take the biometrics after every cross-border mission. Arnab Roy, head of Tunnel, was here himself. They waved, and the MARCOS went to Amjad's room.

'Has he said anything?'

'Nothing. The Tunnel is our only hope.' Amjad returned to the files on his desk, and the MARCOS waited in his office.

Abhimanyu sat quietly in a corner, watching Amjad every few minutes.

He was engrossed into something—a classified file. He looked up.

Abhimanyu looked away.

After almost an hour, Arnab entered. 'Sir, hard disk has been cracked.'

Amjad shut his file and approached the data room.

MARCOS followed him.

It was Sonia's territory. She got on with it immediately. 'It will take time.'

Abhimanyu and Amjad took a break to the cafeteria. Mutual needs trounced their mutual mistrust for now. The television was on. The horrors of the Mumbai attack still reflected on everyone's face on the TV and in the cafeteria. Little did they know of what was yet to come.

'I've been digging. IB's sources are classified. Even for the president.' Amjad broke the silence, but Abhimanyu had a different conversation in mind. Amjad was still his administrative boss.

'It was touch and go.'

Amjad tried to grasp the change in track.

'I don't know how long I can be here.' Abhimanyu looked out the cafeteria window and said it in an uncharacteristic low tone.

At first, Amjad thought it was just a concern. Soon, he realized there was more to it. 'What happened out there?'

Abhimanyu was quiet.

'You have done more, should I say, adventurous missions than this.' Amjad raised his eyebrow.

'I had a team, and their lives depended on my decisions. Also, their family's future. I have completed many missions, but it has never felt like this. It's no longer the same.'

'What do you mean?'

'I mean, it's not adventurous anymore.' Abhimanyu faced him. 'It's a burden.' The harrowing thoughts from when he had been stuck behind that Jeep were all too fresh still. They had turned up ten minutes before time and were almost done for their lives. It dawned on him that everything could have been over in just a second, forever. The margins were always thin, but now they left deep marks behind as well.

'Is it just that?' Amjad found it hard to believe that Abhimanyu Singh Rathore, a veteran, had been bogged down by one near-death experience. He had done way too many missions to fall apart so easily. He had handled bigger responsibilities earlier, bigger team, so the guilt of miscalculations in decisions also didn't make sense. Yes, the afterthoughts happened to everyone, but Abhimanyu had tipped over. Could it be a hangover from their earlier conversation?

For Abhimanyu, there was more to his thoughts, and it went back to the small talk he'd had with Siddhartha in Pasha's safe abode in the desert—the moment of clarity when it dawned on him that he had a personal life which was shaping up beautifully again. In his entire adulthood, he had never felt so much at peace with himself as he now felt around Sasha. A peaceful family life awaited him, just like the one his parents had built for him. For him, it was not just a momentary thought but a rendezvous with his deep-seated desires to have a commoner's life—a life where he'd never have to hide from an unknown enemy, a life where he didn't have to expect the unexpected, a life where he didn't need a plan B and plan C for safety. A normal life.

Abhimanyu realized Amjad couldn't understand his motives and decided it was time to open up and move on. 'I'm tired of breaking in and running away. Tired of killing day in and day out just to survive. I have another shot at a family life, and I want to grab it. You would also agree the two don't go together.' The sacrifices Amjad had made, Abhimanyu wasn't ready to make.

'We can only choose one,' Amjad muttered, clearly still flummoxed by Abhimanyu's thoughts. He nodded sideways to express his disagreement with the decision.

'I've made my choice. It was unthinkable for me two years ago perhaps. Time changes perspective and choices too.'

Amjad took a deep breath. It had nothing to do with the morning talk; there was no game play. He realized he couldn't bring him back. The more he tried, the more it would push him further away. Abhimanyu was in a different zone, so he decided to salvage what he could and keep the mission going. This was not the right time to change the team, let alone the team leader. Besides, at some level, Amjad agreed with him. He'd had an opportunity himself which he'd let go, but, in his loneliness, he often regretted that decision. Amjad knew the longer he pushed it, the more difficult it was to get out. After some time, there was no way out. At times, Abhimanyu was akin to a son to Amjad. Abhimanyu still had age on his side, and his choice was clear. Amjad didn't want to stand in his way. 'If you're so sure, no one can stop you. But you know it well that the mission needs you.'

'But…'

'Finish the mission and you'll be offered an advisory role behind a desk in a godforsaken government department.'

Abhimanyu frowned. 'Far away from Delhi as possible.'

Amjad sweetened the deal more with no response yet. 'All other records will be deleted. You can settle down wherever in India you want.' That was the final cherry.

It was a sweet deal, sweeter than Abhimanyu had expected. He smiled a smile Amjad had never seen in his ten years with Abhimanyu. After all, Abhimanyu was known to be a serious man.

'I have your word?'

'You have my word,' Amjad assured him, to which Abhimanyu flashed a rare ear-to-ear grin.

CHAPTER 14

THE TEAK HOUSE

Abhimanyu laid back in his recliner and stargazed from his room's balcony. To mankind, these were nature's gift, but somewhere in the universe, these stars were just a ball of surging fire. The contrast couldn't have been starker, and it symbolized his current situation too. Suspicion and mistrust belied the calm demeanor he had to maintain on the outside. Even the system looked orderly only on the surface as the moles were burning it hollow. He had to let go of the beauty of the stars and rip it apart to find the prying eyes inside—or find a way to operate beyond the prying eyes.

Reality was far from the idealistic version sold to them in the recruitment days. He surveyed the stars again and felt like a pawn—a prisoner of the institution he had spent his life protecting. It was a carefully structured system to manage chaos and, sometimes, even create chaos. This was not what he had aspired for when he started this journey. They had been told they would be the protectors of human values enshrined in the constitution. They would be the hounds that could cross over and win beyond the ambit of the regular defense institutions. Army, navy, and air force were the first line of defense for the country; they would be the first line of defense for the three of them—the sharp edge of the knife that made it lethal and not the back handle of the knife that held it together. They were supposed to be the bishop of this game, not the pawns.

Frustrated as much as by this falsity of his personal life, he also understood these were extraordinary times for the forces. Institutional mechanisms had failed, his seniors were clueless, and the system had been compromised, perhaps right at the top. MARCOS couldn't be the edge of a knife that had a crack running through its middle. At the same time, a wild tiger couldn't be the keeper of the jungle. He would just not be good at it, just like Pasha's kill was due to his shortcomings. These thoughts invaded his dreams.

In the next room, Akram had his own reasons to worry. The leg wound was not as bad as it had appeared, and he had passed out more because of the excessive morphine than the blood loss. Anymore morphine could have proved fatal. It didn't take the doctor much time to discharge him with a dressing, and he was already walking albeit with a limp after the two-day intensive care. But his wound was not what troubled him. He had seen something very unusual at the border. Abhimanyu had almost frozen. He had taken too long to react when they were pinned behind the Jeep, and any lapse there could have ended it all. It was not the Abhimanyu he knew. Neither did he miss the discomfort between Amjad and Abhimanyu in the morning. It was rare again. Something was up, something important he had no clue about.

Meanwhile, the television was doing what it did the best: drama. Amjad was trying to read every sign in the open. On the backfoot, Pakistanis didn't acknowledge any operation, and Indians postured not just militarily but politically as well. The peace doves on news channels were already questioning the need of such high-risk strategies just when the ties were recovering after the November attacks. Hundred and sixty lives lost in Mumbai didn't matter to them. But then, fifty thousand lives lost in last seventy years didn't matter to them either. Perhaps, in their idyllic utopian world, the idea of protecting a democracy itself didn't matter to them. On the other hand, hawks continued to provide false claims of having avenged the terrorist attacks even though no official on either side had linked the two. Amidst this hara-kiri, it was anybody's guess if the Indian Government could hold off the doves long enough to avert the impending nuclear disaster. The peace lobby was working overtime to avert any further action even though it went against the tide and the mood of the nation. It couldn't be a coincidence. The MARCOS had to make their next move soon. On that thought, Amjad went to sleep too.

Next day, the MARCOS assembled in the lobby. Amjad had messaged them earlier about delay in decryptions. It would take another three days, and he advised them to take leave.

Abhimanyu did not mind a break, but Akram couldn't comprehend it. It seemed the Indians were caving into the media pressure. 'A break in the middle of a mission! Why would you do that?' he confronted Amjad.

'Nothing will happen till we crack the disk. I thought you deserved a break.'

'So, you send us into hibernation even though we're running against a ticking clock?'

'It's not hibernation.'

'What is it?'

Too often, a leave was a prelude to disbanding the team. He knew they had decided to enter Pakistan without keeping the system in the loop, and perhaps it was coming back to bite them.

Abhimanyu sensed Akram's line of thought. 'What we did in Pakistan was brave but not the best. We could have controlled the injuries. We could have kept it lowkey. We could have kept it away from media.' After a moment of contemplation, he continued. 'I think we need a break. I need a break.'

Akram could see fatigue in Abhimanyu's eyes. Things were becoming clearer now. Perhaps that's why Amjad had decided to do it. Perhaps that's what Akram had missed earlier.

Sonia and Siddhartha nodded in agreement, for it had been too much for them too.

'So, I'll go meet Sasha. I suggest you spend some time with your families as well.'

Akram was stumped again. Abhimanyu was not just taking a short break but going all the way back to Assam. The irony didn't skip the others too.

Sonia joked, 'Yeah. I'll go find my future husband too.' After a pause, 'Better be with the codes.'

Satire wasn't lost on Abhimanyu, but he signed off without a retort.

Bagyidaw's Bungalow, Manas River

It was January fourteenth, the first day of festivities of the year—the day of Makar Sankranti. Abhimanyu stood in front of the Bagyidaw's gate with a bouquet he had carried all the way from Delhi. The missing part of his life's puzzle had been fixed in his mind.

Thapa opened the door, only to be startled. 'Did you run away?' Eyes opened wide by surprise.

'Almost.'

'Is it you?' Thapa pointed to the television. The news anchors were all over the cross-border mission.

Abhimanyu couldn't answer but gestured enough for Thapa to guess.

'So, what's the score?'

Abhimanyu smiled, but it was a question that got his adrenaline pumping. Thapa was referring to the number of kills. 'Akram eleven, Siddhartha managed two even with an injury on his first mission, and I did fourteen.'

'This sounds like a unit.'

'Yeah. It's bigger than what any of us have seen.'

'It always is. You can stop there.'

Abhimanyu trusted Thapa more than Thapa was comfortable with. He had taken care of Sasha and had kept her out of sight during these untrustworthy times. Friends are hard to come by, such professionals even harder. While Abhimanyu had snooped for the double agent, Thapa had helped him keep away from them what he held most dear to his heart.

'Where's Sasha?'

'At the teak house, as usual. It's done now, but she loves to keep working on the finishing touches.'

With Abhimanyu back, Thapa hoped the teak house will be finally finished.

Abhimanyu walked to the back yard and noticed the increased security. Army commandos guarded the site, a well-trained cadre with heavy firepower. It looked akin to a Z-level security. The commandos guarded the vulnerable spots of the facility. Though Abhimanyu wondered if they had got the tactics right. Such large bungalows needed patrol teams, not static guards. He couldn't see any patrol. They were protecting the key entry points, but any intruder who observed them for long enough would simply not take those entry points.

He walked through the bushes on the mud path till the top of Sasha's teak house was visible.

Sasha had seen him coming from afar and spontaneously carved the soil there with, *I Love You.*

When Abhimanyu hugged her, he felt her cold body calming his searing heart. 'I'm so happy to see you.'

'Me too.'

He pulled her back.

'How did they leave you?'

Abhimanyu looked away at the clear sky then back at her. 'I'm leaving the services.'

Sasha was stumped.

It certainly wasn't the smile of joy Abhimanyu had expected but an expression of disappointment. 'You don't want that?'

'Yes. No. I mean, I didn't expect it.'

Abhimanyu could read her mind. As much as the thought pleased her, perhaps she wondered if he could really relinquish the identity that had defined him for so many years and still be happy. 'I'll be fine.'

To Sasha, it was more than that. She knew the sheer passion, grit, and perseverance Abhimanyu had put into building this world. For him to move beyond it, for her, wasn't comforting at all. Nevertheless, she hugged him to show her support in what he had already decided.

*****

The prying eyes in Delhi had followed him to Bagyidaw's. Amjad had requested the Intelligence Bureau's satellite command put a twenty-four/seven tag on him. 'He's not coming back,' Amjad said, staring at the screen. Amjad couldn't hear anything but could see enough even through the satellite's distorted pixels. Sasha's *I Love You* was visible enough from the sky. Amjad was personally happy but professionally hurt. It was clear to the stars, as was to Amjad, he had lost his prodigy.

*****

'You have a knack to surprise.' Sasha held his hand.

'And you too.' He eyed the soil carvings. 'How did you know I was coming?'

Sasha laughed. 'Behold, thy spymaster. You're talking to the communications director of the Bagyidaw's mansion security.'

Abhimanyu was surprised to realize she had access to the communications room. Thapa was not one of those.

'Let me show you.' She pulled his hand and took him to her citadel. 'The communications room. I can monitor anything approaching the mansion from a mile.'

He looked around, for even he had never visited this room before. 'So, Thapa gave you your toys.'

'Yes, I believe I'm skillful.'

'She has been doing a good job on the communications systems. I'm just happy I don't have to pay her.' Thapa joined them.

Abhimanyu was beginning to understand the changes now. 'Why do we have so much security?' he asked Thapa.

'Let's get some food. You've just arrived. We don't need to discuss everything right now.' Thapa dodged it but knew Abhimanyu would be persistent, so he added, 'I'll brief you on everything later.'

The lovebirds were free to nest. Sasha smiled and acknowledged the favor. However, she knew it wouldn't be long before they'd have to apprise him of the situation and the threats they had received.

January 15, 2009

India decided to have only one time zone despite the thirty-two-hundred-kilometer longitudinal distance between east and west. It meant the sun usually set early in this part of the country—sometimes as early as 5:30 p.m., which was the case today. The sun was about to set on Bagyidaw's. After a sumptuous lunch, the deep afternoon was a welcomed errand, not to mention last night's long sleep.

Abhimanyu, well and truly, had recovered on all the rest deficit. The window was open, and an image in the far horizon distracted him. He thought he had seen rays of light, perhaps a bonfire in the eastern hills. No known village was there. He gently slid from bed without disturbing Sasha. The light could just have been the moonlight's reflection off the hills, but curiosity got the better of him. He sneaked through the Z-security layer without a fuss and into the jungles surrounding the Bagyidaw's bungalow. Abhimanyu walked through the jungle mud path armed with only a torchlight and minimal accessories in his pockets, including a Swiss knife, night googles, and a single Glock.

Tall trees and bushes all around would make it easy for anyone to hide in the jungles. Besides, outsized security arrangements only meant Thapa and Sasha were hiding something. The anomaly had activated his sixth sense.

With the kind of security Bagyidaw's had, no one would brave attacking the compound without observing it for long enough. And, for that, they would have to hide somewhere nearby; Abhimanyu had to just find those trails. He used the darkness to sneak through the jungle without any fuss. He cut through the shrubs and the trees with his Swiss knife and scouted for possible hiding spots—perhaps behind a group of clustered trees or under its huge trunks, perhaps on top of the branches of wide base trees or any dark caverns. If a threat existed nearby, indeed it had to hide in these places. After an hour of treading through the jungles, Abhimanyu had found nothing. He started to think it was just his paranoia.

Maybe he should have just confronted Thapa and Sasha. Finally, he reached the banks of the Kopili River. The noisy stream calmed down only at the Umrangso Lake, many miles downstream. This was a good spot to stop for a break.

Abhimanyu checked under the rocks, next to the trees, and beside the waterline. If any fire spots had existed, they had been washed away. A little farther ahead, tall, clustered woods lined the riverbanks. He spotted a small log, almost finished, entangled in the river shrub and refusing to get pulled in by the water stream. Abhimanyu picked it up and gently tapped it against the rock. It broke off with little force. Someone had used it in a fire, but it was only half burnt. Abhimanyu pressed the broken half between his fingers. He could feel the ash which had coagulated with water in the brittle wood crevices. But this wasn't enough. It could have been anyone. He needed a more specific lead.

Abhimanyu noticed a low sound from the river—a flapping every time the wind blew to west. He couldn't see anything though, so he folded his pants and entered the river. Abhimanyu kneeled while tapping carefully to ensure he didn't step on a crab or a thorn fish. Finally, he saw it—a half-burnt piece of paper. With a delicate hand, he pulled it out. But Abhimanyu couldn't read anything. The paper was intact, but water had erased most of the ink marks. Only a few patterns remained. Whoever had used it must have not gone far. He removed his gun.

Abhimanyu scanned the paper. He had to find someone who could read it but had no link to the agency. He thought for a moment and clicked a snapshot. Abhimanyu relayed it on his personal chat to Mrs. Rituparno Sen, a professor of Jadavpur University. He had met her during a leadership training program, and she had been a handful of resource ever since. As a professor fluent in multiple languages, she could decode regional languages at the blink of an eye. University was her day job. As a fierce nationalist, she took special pride in helping Abhimanyu even without the public recognition. It was a different matter that they had also been involved romantically during the duration of the course. However, before things took a serious turn, they had decided to call it off. It had been amply clear they couldn't live in each other's life. Friendship was their best bet.

Abhimanyu used RAW's secure chat service, Ericsson. It was a handy tool to establish anonymous IP. The servers were designed to isolate each team module with cyber walls. Sonia managed it for their team, and it was the safest line to use now. Only they would have access to the chats.

Rituparno didn't make him wait with a reply. *It's Urdu paper with a few names on it. Can't make out everything, but they read Hussain, Akbar, Allah-uddin in parts.* Then came the shocker.

There is also a full line which reads something like cort … stat but I can't make sense of it, as most of it has been wiped off.

Abhimanyu needed to read no further. Cort could easily mean Cortex, which is all he wanted to know. Question wasn't who were they but what were they doing here?

His paranoia had turned into reality. Lost in his thoughts, Abhimanyu turned to return to the bungalow. His only company through this lone walk were the stars. His vision in the northeast blurred. The stars wobbled strangely. Was it smoke? He noticed the pattern of the blur. It was definitely smoke, and he zeroed in on the hills farther in the north. It could only be the tribal or the intruders. Abhimanyu decided to verify for his own peace of mind. He walked toward the hills, feet pressed hard, ears alert to every noise, and eyes probing the jungle for traps. If it were terrorists, they would definitely take some precautionary measures.

As he approached the hills, the blur in the sky thickened. Orion's belt was waving wildly. A commoner's eye couldn't spot it, but a trained eye couldn't miss it either. Someone had definitely lit a fire in the safety of the hills. Abhimanyu kept moving forward. A chatter of sound was faintly audible now. It was still too far to understand the language, but he could hear four or five people talking. This was no camping ground, so only hideaways were to be found here. Even the nearest farms would be at least fifty kilometers. He now wished he had carried more bullets. At least he had his night goggles. He was not far now; their voices grew much louder. He could hear words like, "Janaab, Shukriya, Dua, and Rehmat." It was a dialect of Urdu. He deduced it was Sindhi Urdu, popular in Pakistan. Abhimanyu unlocked his Glock.

He manuevered through the wild shrubs and noticed an unnatural bent in the towering semals. Something was pulling down the tall tree. He scanned the tree to the roots, and, thanks to his night goggles, he spotted the very thin silver straight line of an aluminum thread barely visible even during daytime. The moonlight did the trick. He followed the thread and turned around the trunk of at least five other trees. Abhimanyu scratched one of the trunks; it smelled RDX. The tree trunks were loaded with RDX. These men were not messing around. Abhimanyu carefully navigated the wires and emerged on the cuesta. From this height, he could see them at a distance of about fifty meters. Abhimanyu mounted his silencer on to the gun's muzzle. He spotted one of them sitting on a tree, guarding for intruders rather than sleeping. Perhaps no one had ever come this way. That's probably why Abhimanyu wasn't spotted. He couldn't see the faces, but he counted four of them sitting around the fire. Abhimanyu hid behind the thickest trunk nearby and waited for the right moment.

He had to neutralize them before they could reach for their guns, which were lying by the rocks a few meters farther. Only one of them had his semi-automatic gun with him. He had a towel around his neck and seemed like the group leader. Abhimanyu had to take him out and destroy his gun. Other men would inevitably run toward their guns. He calculated he would have perhaps eight to ten seconds to take aim at them before they could reach their guns. Before any of that, he would also have to shoot down the watcher in the tree. Abhimanyu realized he didn't have enough time or ammunition to take them on. They were just too many.

They finished their meals and laid on the fireside, not yet off to sleep. Abhimanyu waited. Few minutes later, they were still half alert and continued in Sindhi Urdu. The elder one was telling tales of how he had killed Americans, Russians, and Indians in his young days. All of Abhimanyu's doubts were now cleared. These were fedayeen who had somehow reached this part of the country. The Indian intelligence couldn't have missed this kind of an intel. The guards were to protect the compound from fedayeen.

He sent an SOS to Thapa from his mobile. *Fedayeen in jungles. Get men at the cliff by the riverside.*

Abhimanyu checked his cargos to find he only had a few cannisters and a couple magazines. He turned to sit but inadvertently stepped on dry leaves. Unfortunately, at that moment, even the jungle noise was at its minimal. The crackling of leaves were heard distinctly, an aberration to the night's rhythm.

One fedayeen heard it and alerted another one.

'An animal?' He reluctantly woke up.

'Could be. Let me check. Give me cover.' The fedayeen stood and waited for his sleepy colleague to gain full conscious. He handed him the gun and walked toward the sound.

Abhimanyu could feel his footsteps approaching him. It was the worst-case scenario. There was no way he could escape their eyes for long enough. Thapa and his team would still take some time to reach there. Abhimanyu's hands were forced now.

Eventually, Abhimanyu decided to take his shot. He slid behind another tree at a better angle to the shooter on the treetop. It would give him the best cover and visibility. Abhimanyu threw a small smoke can toward the tree to blunt the shooter's vision. The smoke rose, and he double tapped the fedayeen approaching him, who died instantly without a groan.

The fedayeen giving him cover was shaken from his sleep now. He fired back on reflex with his semiautomatic machinegun.

Others took a few seconds before realizing someone was sniping at them and running toward their guns.

Abhimanyu aimed at them and fired a few shots. But the fedayeen had spotted him, and his Glock couldn't counter the submachine gun. Abhimanyu took heavy fire from the shooter at top as well.

The shooter couldn't see him but fired sporadically nevertheless. He wasn't worried about wasting ammunition.

Abhimanyu had a ten-millimeter automatic gun firing at him at a speed of not less than two hundred rounds per minute. It was akin to a fighter aircraft gun barrel. He was taken aback by their firepower so deep inside India. A gun like this could only be found with the military, would be heavy to carry, and very difficult to hide. Local insurgents and even fedayeen usually carried Kalashnikovs or MI automatics at the most. One run in Abhimanyu's direct line would be enough to shred apart the tree and kill him. Abhimanyu realized he was heavily outmatched. At the next refill, he crawled to the next tree. Abhimanyu wasn't carrying his flash stopper, and the tree trooper had spotted the gun flash by now. He targeted the tree and took it out in the first run, as expected. Abhimanyu wasn't equipped to fight this kind of firepower. Desperate for an escape, he changed his plan. He crawled under the bushes and out of the fire zone.

The tree trooper was still scanning the jungle to spot him, and the three other men were coming for him on foot.

Abhimanyu checked his cargo pockets. He had one more smoke cannister, one grenade, and one cartridge file left—barely enough to camouflage an escape. He recalled the river cliff. If only he could make it to the rock shelter there … Darkness was his only ally now.

Foot troopers were almost onto him. He removed the pin on his smoke-only grenade and threw it toward the gunmen. They took cover, and he dashed toward the river.

The tree trooper could only see the smoke, so he again fired indiscriminately.

A few bullets whisked past Abhimanyu's ears. The husky sound of bullets was heavy, and he couldn't mistake it to anything else. They were trained for it. He knew he was lucky to have missed it. Abhimanyu kept running; he could see the river now. But his legs buckled, and before he could grasp what had happened, he smelled soil in his face. Blood leaked from his calf muscles. The tree trooper had managed a hit. His pain was unbearable, and he wasn't carrying any painkillers. He tightened the cargo pants around the wound as a makeshift tourniquet to at least slow the bleeding.

Abhimanyu tried to run but couldn't. He heard the fedayeen moving in the trees. They were coming for him. His vision blurred due to heavy blood loss. He needed to buy a little more time. Abhimanyu unpinned his last grenade and threw it into the trees toward the fedayeen. It blew with a flash that struck Abhimanyu like a bolt. He saw a face he had been looking for, for years—his archfoe, Hussain Qadir, the satan, the meloch, the prince of his darkness, the man who had killed Bhavya, his first wife. A deep desire for revenge surged through his veins, but his body failed to respond. He checked again for any more ammunition, but there was none except the lone magazine in the Glock. Abhimanyu didn't stand a chance. After a few moments of despair, Abhimanyu calmed himself. Reality sunk into him soon. He had to survive today, to end it all tomorrow. The fedayeen were still not dead, for he heard them moving and checking for others. He had to hide soon. Thapa and his men should not be far off by now.

Abhimanyu was struggling to maintain his balance but lowered his body on the cliff just enough to hang from the rock. With one painful swing, he threw his body into the gap under the rock. Upon landing, his pain surged instantly. It cracked through his body. Abhimanyu groaned involuntarily, but the noise was muzzled thanks to the flash fire from the grenade blast. The river underneath the cliff was calm, but the bend farther down made its presence known through the constant splattering. Abhimanyu tried to avoid any more sounds. His eyes were still red with pain and a longing desire to avenge Bhavya's death. Abhimanyu closed his eyes and warped his visions into the dark night.

*****

Thapa couldn't believe the message. How could Abhimanyu be so foolish to venture alone into the jungles? Perhaps it wasn't Abhimanyu's mistake alone. After all, none of them had shared anything about the threats they had received. Thapa took couple commando groups with him and left the rest to guard the Bagyidaw's. Sasha was longing to join, but Thapa didn't allow her. Besides, he needed someone in the communication room.

As they went deeper into the jungles, they could hear sporadic gunfire and even a couple of blasts. Thapa realized Abhimanyu was definitely in a soup. Thankfully, his commandos were loaded lock, stock, and barrel. They even carried medical aid should anyone, especially Abhimanyu, need it.

The commandos probed and foraged through the woods, one view at a time. The two commando groups spread out horizontally in a wall formation to cover as much area as possible. But their torchlights were still in pocket, for no one wanted to reveal their position to any lurking danger.

Sasha followed them through the drone and provided them air cover. She had tagged the location of grenade flash and used the GPS to guide the commandos. They kept walking in that direction.

'Do you smell that?' Alpha 1 team leader asked.

'Gunpowder,' another commando replied.

'The sight is still farther down the slope.'

'But I can smell it. Something happened here.'

Soon, they arrived at the riverbank.

'This is a grenade crater. Fresh.' A commando kneeled to feel the warm ash where Abhimanyu had thrown his last grenade.

They split into pairs and extinguished the torchlights. They moved around in calibrated maneuvers, trained akin to a cat's movement in the darkness.

Thapa moved toward the river and spotted the grenade pin. He looked for the fine markings. It was a MARCOS grenade. 'Abhimanyu was here.'

The commandos searched everywhere but found no one in the jungles. The fedayeen had cleared even the ash from the bonfire.

'Careful.' A commando held Thapa as he walked up to look down.

He couldn't see anything at first. Then something. Thapa used the night goggles to see a human body lying motionless under the rock. He kneeled. 'It's him.' Thapa's heartbroken voice said everything loud and clear. He could barely hold the sight of the blood loss.

They slipped down the ridge with the help of a rope tied to the thick semal tree trunk and pulled him out slowly and rushed him to the Bagyidaw's.

Over the next few hours, Thapa gave him first aid and even transfused blood. They needed to buy time till he could be taken to the military hospital in Guwahati. Luckily, a commando had the same blood type.

Thanks to Thapa's efforts, Abhimanyu finally opened his eyes, and his first words were, 'Get me Amjad.' He had seen a paper referencing Cortex. He had seen fedayeen. He had seen Hussain Qadir. He had seen too much.

'You need some rest first. Let's talk tomorrow morning,' Sasha said sternly, as she had a task now—to stop this forever.

As for Abhimanyu, he had a lot more to chase, a lot more to protect. The enemy was getting personal and closer to his family more than ever before.

January 17, 2009

Abhimanyu woke on a stiff bed. The clock read just past nine. The bed's wooden planks rested on a steel frame barely supporting his weight. The beds in military hospitals were of the cheapest quality the local command could afford. The bureaucrats thought never gave enough pennies for such *peacetime frivolity*, as they called it. Abhimanyu was in the general ward, but it was empty except for a few security men standing next to his bed.

Thapa stood at the end of his bed and smiled.

Doctors had been working on him for over twenty-four hours. After a significant blood transfusion, his body had moved into the recovery mode, and he had been transferred from the ICU. His legs were still plastered toe to knee, but Thapa was happy to see him gain conscious.

'Do you know who they were?' Abhimanyu hadn't forgotten about Qadir lest be taken for insanity.

No Pakistani agent had come this far inside the country yet, unless they had already figured it out.

Thapa thought for a moment and shook his head. 'Local insurgents to stay around. I have an agreement with them. We don't disturb them, and they don't disturb us.'

'So, they have never attacked the bungalow?'

Thapa again shook his head. 'Never. If they've ventured so far into the jungles, its generally because they need help for themselves—sometimes with rations, sometimes with petrol or even just money. I've helped them occasionally, so no local group has targeted us. We have got stuck in cross firing between rival insurgent groups a few times but never an attack on us.'

'Do the local insurgents speak Urdu?'

'It's rare, but some of the Muslim refugees, Rohingyas from Myanmar, do speak it. But, again, none of them come this far and disturb us. Even the bravest of the insurgents never cross the river.'

Abhimanyu didn't mention anything about Cortex or the Urdu paper. 'Where are my cargos?'

'Locked in my room.'

The paper was safe, he thought. Thapa was the only one he trusted at this point. Still, he double checked on him, asked him a few more questions, for Abhimanyu had the instincts to catch a lie even from the hospital bed. Thapa wasn't lying. 'That's comforting. We need to reinforce the security.'

Thapa nodded dutifully. While it wasn't direct, Thapa was smart enough to understand where Abhimanyu was going. He held his composure and changed the tack. 'Amjad has been waiting to talk to you.' Thapa had handled many agents in his lifetime and was party to many secrets. He knew the ways of the spies. He also knew it left them alone to face the darkness in their life. Their instincts of mistrust creeped into every relationship and often controlled their lives. Thapa dialed Amjad on a secure wireless line for him.

'Thank you, Thapa.' Abhimanyu's tone meant only one thing for Thapa and the soldiers.

They immediately left him alone for his call with Amjad.

Abhimanyu couldn't take anything for granted when it came to his family. Thapa had provided Sasha a safe refuge in the Bagyidaw's bungalow, but Abhimanyu was still struggling with trusting him completely. He wondered if Amjad could get him some answers. But, again, he couldn't even trust Amjad with everything he knew. Time was his only friend.

The phone rang. 'You can't take a holiday, can you?' Amjad spoke on speaker.

Abhimanyu covered his mouth even though no one was in the room now. 'I saw something. I think I'm onto something.'

'Yes, just like you thought you wanted to retire.' Amjad wished to remind him that his commando instincts would never leave him. They would always hang over him.

'Is this line secure?'

'As secure as it can be.'

Abhimanyu finally dropped his guard. 'I found a paper written in Urdu. It had Cortex mentioned on it.'

Amjad was taken aback. 'How did a paper like that surface randomly in a northeast jungle?'

'Exactly. It can't be a coincidence.' Abhimanyu had played his only card.

'Of course not.' Amjad pondered it. 'You've been in the spotlight for quite some time. Now we have Khalid, thanks to you. They're trying to get at you.'

Abhimanyu listened carefully. He had a different track of conversation on his mind, but this was also important.

'I half expect that, but you seem to be hundred percent confident.' Amjad didn't want to do this on a phone, but he had no choice.

'Am I missing something?'

After deliberating on the right choice of words, Amjad answered him. 'Listen, we didn't tell you, since you were on a mission, but Thapa and Sasha got a threatening letter sometime back. We immediately tightened the security at Bagyidaw's. All those commandos there are not for you. They're to protect Sasha.'

Abhimanyu didn't trust Amjad already. Now he couldn't hate him enough too. He soaked in the silence for a few moments till his left brain intervened. If he was in Amjad's place, he would have done the same. Amjad had done the best he could in that situation. But there was one problem. 'Your commandos are uninitiated.'

'They are the best from the army's northeastern command.'

'Exactly. We don't need the army infantry to outsmart the terrorists. They won't break in with a gunfight. They will sneak in.'

Amjad saw the point.

'These soldiers, good as they are, don't stand a chance if they eventually decide to come.'

For Amjad, only one solution existed. 'I'll send in MARCOS, best of the lot.'

That was more than Abhimanyu had expected. He had just thought of training a few army commandos his way.

'Let me know the names of who you trust,' Amjad added, really stretching his resources and trying to help. Amjad would need the highest permissions to spare any MARCO.

Abhimanyu felt obliged but stopped short of acknowledging it and regained his composure. 'I'll just need a team of three. They can train the rest. I'm sure they'll make the best use of the commandos we already have here.'

'They'll fly in by tonight.'

'I guess I owe you one.'

'Don't think about it. Just get well soon and come back because we need you. Doctor tells me the wounds are very local. With the right medication and rest, you should be fine in three to four days.'

Abhimanyu eyed the plasters which told a different story but chose to ignore it. His mind was focused on the mission now. 'How's Siddhartha's recovery?'

'Quite well. Should be fine before you. Sonia is passing some free time with her team, and Akram is just relaxing in Aligarh.'

'Has Khalid given away anything yet?' Abhimanyu realized he should have started with this question. It would be tough to break his brain.

'Not much. Just enough to stay alive. Smart cookie. We'll need to do something unorthodox.'

'The disk?'

'Coders are on it. Let's see.' If they still had not cracked the disk, they would have already tried everything on Khalid's mind, yet they were nowhere. 'We'll have enough soon. It's just a matter of time.'

'That's all we don't have—time.'

Things were moving too fast, and Abhimanyu was beginning to believe they were up against a clock, just that they hadn't found it yet. A night's adventure—rather, misadventure—had resulted in some delay, but even if the fedayeen were here to attack the compound, they had paid a heavy price. They had been flushed out of the area, surveillance had been tightened, and security would not be an issue anymore. With his family secure, he could go after them with vengeance.

IB Headquarters, January 18

The cold wind from the Himalayas covered vast horizons of New Delhi in thick smog that choked the traffic for the weekend savvy Delhites. A similar smog had befallen the Indian Intelligence too, and they were desperate to lift the smokescreen.

Amjad drove through it to reach the bureau headquarters albeit a bit late. Shankar had finally heeded to his request for a stimulated interrogation. The subject would have to endure repeated aversive stimuli beyond their control. The interrogation team had already primed him for the last two days.

Khalid had relinquished any semblance of control. They knew it when he had decided not to run away even when the guard had left his cell open the previous night.

Khalid had stayed inside the cell, for he had realized escape was futile.

It was time for the last nail in the coffin now, and Shankar had chosen Sunaina to do it. She had a reputation for interrogations and was most likely the best at it amongst the senior personnel's at the agency. Sunaina was unhappy with the way Amjad had dealt with her a few days ago.

He entered the room and braced for some bitterness. 'We're all set.'

Shankar was there before him, thankfully. He sat in the head chair. Indians had thrown every known conventional technique at Khalid, but his mind was just too strong. It forced them to shift gear to psych-ops—a dirty word in public. The technique was all about priming his brain to accept that he had no choice but to adhere to any command the Indians gave him. It included drugging him, offering food only after he had finished a preset sequence of physically strenuous tasks, depriving him of sleep till his eyes were swollen and blood red. The list went on. Even for a brain like his, it took just two days to turn compliant.

'Here's the script.' Shankar handed it to her.

Sunaina sat across from Amjad. Their eyes locked, and Amjad saw no awkwardness. She smiled, and Amjad duly returned it. It was a good sign, for Amjad needed to be on the right side of the Border Intelligence now.

At Shankar's cue, they followed him to the basement and sat in a minivan painted in the colors of a food delivery van—a necessary disguise to break the trail to Khalid. The minivan left the Intelligence Bureau headquarters from its back gate at the regular food delivery time. The driver followed the route to the kitchen and, only twenty minutes later, took a detour. After an hour, abandoned open-pit mines appeared on the sides. They had almost arrived. Soon, they were inside the Asola wildlife sanctuary. The van drove through the sanctuary's mud paths till it arrived at a set of two houses in the deep jungles. The Bhadkal lake, an important source of water for Delhi, stood still in the background. It was a quite night, only so far. They went to the observation room.

Amjad smiled at Sunaina and opened the door.

She struggled to smile back. Perhaps it was the stress of the interrogation.

'Take it easy.' Amjad passed her a bottle of water.

Khalid was pinned to the chair with his hands tied and eyes blindfolded. He hadn't given away anything yet, and it was the Indians who were on edge now. They had to make this work at any cost.

'We've been trying the wrong things on him. He has a very strong mind, a PhD from MIT after all. But he doesn't have an equally strong body.'

Shankar and Amjad took their positions in the observation room while Sunaina moved into the interrogation room. The guards closed the door. It was dark, with a slight ventilation. The sun rays through the ventilation fell directly on Khalid's face.

Sunaina nodded at the guard.

He pulled a glass shutter at the ventilation to increase the light intensity and removed Khalid's blindfold.

Khalid was rendered unsighted for the first few seconds. 'Water.' He looked around desperately. They hadn't given him any liquids in the last two days. His body yearned for just one touch of the Adam's ale.

'You like water?'

Khalid nodded respectfully. He searched for the face behind the voice, but no light shone on Sunaina, though she sat right across the table.

'Khalid, will you comply?'

He looked at where the voice had come from and nodded abjectly. From stress, Khalid sweated effusively, not good for a dehydrated body.

'I will help you with water, but before that, you must help me with some questions.'

Khalid looked away from the voice, perhaps looking to bury his head in sand.

'Will you?'

Khalid stayed quiet.

'For every right answer, I'll offer you a capful of water.'

He looked up at the voice. His eyes were almost knocked out.

Sunaina repeated sternly, 'Will you?'

He stared at the voice and nodded obediently.

'Here we go.' Shankar's anxiety was only little less than Amjad's.

'Tell me the name of your kids.'

'Ayan and Riyan.' He was telling the truth. That was a check question, and Sunaina could move to the next level. She would have to slowly rely more on his body cues.

'Who's your wife, and what does she do?'

'Rukhsana. She died.'

The Indian Intelligence already knew it. The crosschecks had ensured the subject was indeed primed. His drugged eyes were also moist now.

Sunaina saw an opening. 'How did she die?'

Khalid looked away from the voice. A teardrop rolled down his cheek, for he hadn't spoken of it with anyone, though it was the cause of all his guilt. 'I killed her.'

'What?'

'Yes, I killed her.'

'Why?'

'Because she knew too much.'

Sunaina leaned forward into the light. 'Too much about what?'

His neck twitched. Khalid was panicking. Stress was taking a toll on him.

Sunaina grew worried about his red face, which was fluttering to the left, away from the light. 'Okay, leave it. Take some water.' She offered him a glassful.

He lunged at it with force, but the chains restrained him, yanking him back.

Sunaina was scared for a moment, but the guard entered, held Khalid's mouth open and offered him water sip by sip.

'We need to probe further, Sunaina.' Shankar thought they were onto something, but Sunaina was anxious to probe further.

After Khalid calmed down, she resumed the script. 'How long have you been working in the Pakistani Army?'

'Twenty-five years.'

'Right after you graduated MIT?'

'No, I worked as a professor for five years. Then I joined the army.'

'Why did you join the army?'

Khalid was quiet again.

Sunaina leaned forward into the light and repeated her question.

He eyed the voice and said nothing.

Sunaina signaled the guard, and he tightened the chains behind his hands. The chair had acupressure pins at the back, and the sensation was quite comforting at first, until it was pressed against the back for long and turned terribly painful.

Khalid groaned.

Sunaina repeated the question.

'To serve God. He gave me the command, and I obeyed it.' The illusion was trustworthy for a religious soldier but not for a professional. Sunaina knew he was telling the truth.

'Tell me, Khalid, do you know anything about Cortex?'

His eyes widened. It was the first time during the interrogation he had responded to that name. He nodded.

'What do you know about it?'

He tried to speak, but the words wouldn't come out. The sweat on his face was visible to even Amjad and Shankar across the glass wall.

'I hope the stress doesn't break him before we break him,' Amjad said, concerned.

'I cannot.'

Sunaina leaned back, exasperated. Khalid was not stalling, but it was something new.

'Try it politely. We need a name, Sunaina.' Shankar said in her earpiece.

'Why, Khalid?'

'God will punish me.'

Something struck her. For the first time, it appeared as if God was not God but someone specific, someone Khalid knew in flesh. She leaned forward and asked him again, 'Who is your God?'

Light from the ventilation turned toward her as the sun went down the hole. This time, her face had a ray of light.

Finally, Khalid had a face for the voice commanding him. Khalid had not engaged in any serious human interaction in the last forty-eight hours. Khalid leaned forward, studied her chest and smiled.

'Is he going mad?' Amjad asked. 'I won't be surprised, given the dosages.'

'You mean Allah?' Sunaina asked; perhaps it was all along the God.

Khalid smiled again. 'Allah is kind. Not this one.'

She was getting frustrated. 'Who is your God, Khalid?'

He mumbled something Sunaina couldn't discern then said, 'My hands.'

'What happened to your hands?'

'They are burning.' Khalid's smile had disappeared. 'I can't feel my hands. Can you open them?'

Sunaina was confused. 'Please!'

'It's okay. Open them,' Shankar prompted her. The interrogation was taking its toll on Khalid, and Shankar didn't want to lose him altogether. They couldn't kill the hen that would lay the golden egg.

The guard opened the cuffs and stood between the two of them.

'Water.'

The guard offered him a glass full.

Khalid drank it one sip at a time. With every sip, he looked sharper. A glass of water seemed to have done him a lot of good. Khalid kept the glass closer to Sunaina. 'It's a nice shirt.'

Sunaina was surprised. He didn't look like a man under stress now. 'Thank you. Now you need to answer me, Khalid.'

Khalid pulled out his hands that carried red spots of inflammations and flakes from dehydration, stretched them and put them firmly on the table. He nodded. 'I was just a professor when I met him.'

Sunaina had finally done it. She leaned forward in excitement, her face almost upon Khalid's face now. 'So, he is a person?'

Khalid was quiet. He looked toward the ventilation. Something had distracted his attention.

The guard looked at him, surprised, and turned toward the ventilation by reflex.

In that split moment, Khalid's hand stretched out, and before Sunaina could react, he pulled her pen from her shirt.

The guard turned back at the first noise of the movement, but it was already too late. He saw Khalid's hands at her chest and lunged forward to retract it. The guard held Sunaina, who was in shock.

Khalid was completely in control, and nothing could explain that action.

But, in trying to hold Sunaina's balance, the guard had lost precious seconds on Khalid.

Khalid plunged the pointed end of the pen into his jugular vein. Blood poured from it. In a matter of moments, the floor was blood soaked, and Khalid was dead.

Amjad and Shankar rushed to the interrogation room and switched on the lights. Despair and gloom had befallen them.

His eyes were wide open, as if caught dead in the headlights. All their efforts of the past weeks had been flushed down the drain in a single moment of madness.

Sunaina was in complete shock, and Amjad held her to no avail, even as the in-house doctor rushed in to announce the fated, 'He is dead.'

The reality sunk in, and the Indian Intelligence top brass stood there, gasping for any grip on the circumstances.

'Why?' Shankar held his head in his hand. 'I thought we had him under control.'

His eyes said a story of its own.

Amjad closed them. 'Fear.' Amjad regarded Shankar. 'We need to find his source of fear.'

Shankar looked at those eyes.

As the doctor bagged the body, their shoulders dropped. The despondent look on all their faces said it all, that they had lost their only lead to the source.

CHAPTER 15

DUTY CALL

IB Headquarters, January 19

Amjad lifted the paperweight. It was gifted to him on the successful completion of the Chennai mission in 2006 by none other than the current NSA himself. Amjad played with it to release stress but to no avail. It felt heavier between his fingers today. Another similar mission was taking its toll on them as the pieces of the puzzle refused to add up. The agency was already under severe media scrutiny. An exceptional officer and an exceptional informant had been lost to a rigged decision. The hard disk refused to yield much, and their most important lead, Khalid, was dead. To top it all, his lead commando had his sights set on retirement—never a good omen in middle of a mission. The institution he led was breaking down.

Amjad reviewed the list of MARCOS he had prepared for Abhimanyu's replacement. In his heart, he wasn't comfortable with any of them. Not many had worked on a nuclear attack in the past. The situation was now escalating quickly, and the prime minister's office were preparing scenarios for a potential catastrophic failure. In desperation, he dialed Sonia, who was back with the coders and working on the disk. 'Have you settled in?'

'Yes. I've been trying to understand what happened to this disk.'

'What do you mean?'

Sonia paused. 'Do you think it's possible for someone … to mishandle the disk?'

'Mishandle?'

'Tamper. Corrupt.'

Amjad stared into the abyss. The walls were closing in too fast. 'I wouldn't disregard that doubt completely.'

'In that case, I feel the disk has been tampered. Few indices are missing.'

'English, please?'

'When you delete data in your laptop or hard disk, the OS typically only changes the pointers to the data. Each file has a pointer which acts as the address of the data bytes on the hard disk. It tells your operating system the start and the end of the data.'

'Go on. I'm tracking.'

'When you delete a file, the operating system only deletes the pointers and marks those sectors to be written over in the future. We have discovered a sequence of pointers missing from the overall sequence. And how is that possible, unless …?'

'Unless someone has deleted data from the disk. Can you pinpoint when the indexed data went missing?'

'We did the digital trace analysis already. It's been erased in the last week.'

Amjad took a moment to digest that. He couldn't leave anything to chance, for the many implications it had. 'Can you explain more?'

'I meant the data sectors from which the files are deleted belong to the part of hard disk which was written earliest. Normally, hard disks write linearly in one direction, so the earlier in sequence your data is, the older it is. That is, of course, unless the data was deleted then overwritten, which would lead to deindexing. But every time you delete and rewrite a data sector, it leaves behind digital traces. These traces are often enough to tell how far back the files have been deleted, since they are indexed. Depending on the system, it can be a month or a year. It is never day dated.'

'So, you can't give me the date but month maybe of when it was deleted?'

'Yes. It was deleted this month.'

'The disk has been everywhere this month. Remember, it came to us only last week.'

'But the digital traces are very detailed—fresh. The software can't pass that judgement, but I know when I am looking at it. These have been generated within the last week, not just the last month. I can't prove it to you, but that's what my experience says.'

Amjad had known Sonia long enough to know her own analysis was never wrong. She had a reputation for it. It meant two MARCOS had spoken to him about a mole, separately. He could not wait to act on it anymore. 'Have you spoken to Abhimanyu about it yet?'

'No, why?'

'He has a similar theory. He thinks someone within our network is helping the terrorists—a mole.'

Even though Sonia was implying the same, she was appalled, because she hadn't expected to be taken seriously. She hadn't taken herself seriously. But two different people had arrived at the same hypothesis. The probability was not just twice but exponentially double. While she reckoned with the probabilities, her heart dreaded the prospects of a mole. It wouldn't be easy to circumvent a mole at this stage of the operation. 'We should act on it, now.' A steely determination replaced the dreadful fear of a mole in her eyes.

Amjad dialed in Abhimanyu. 'Are you alone?'

'Give me a second.' Abhimanyu checked outside his door and even windows. He saw no one but a commando guarding the house far from his room's door. He closed the door without a sound. 'All alone.'

'Sonia has discovered that the hard disk has missing indices, and based on the digital traces, it has been done recently.'

'How recent?'

'Very recent. Last week or so. It means your theory could be right. The mole is perhaps more resourceful than you or I had thought. He found a way to the hard disk.'

Abhimanyu sat on the chair, hand on his mouth. 'It tells us at least one thing. He is certainly not an IT expert. Perhaps an administrative employee who could have access to the evidence room. No tech savvy person will forget to take care of digital traces.' Abhimanyu's mind was as sharp as ever even though he was still recovering.

Amjad eyed Sonia to check if that made sense.

'It's not as simple as that. But yes, if the person has managed his way to the hard disk, we should expect him to be adept at destroying all trails.'

All it meant was Abhimanyu felt vindicated. 'Oh, I wish I was there. I finally have your ears, Amjad.'

Amjad saw a little ray of light even in this dire situation, for he could sense the soldier in Abhimanyu hadn't faded yet.

'Did you check the evidence room logs?'

'There are many senior people who don't need to log their entry,' Amjad interrupted Abhimanyu's line of thought. 'How's your recovery?' Amjad needed Abhimanyu to be in the field again.

'Quite good. A bit of pain here and there, but I can walk and even run a bit now. The nurse says a few more days of rest and I can be mission fit.'

Things were escalating, and Amjad needed his brain in the control room if not in the field. 'In that case, why don't you come here now? Delhi has the best doctors anyway.'

'I know it's your way to get the work done, Amjad.'

Amjad let it sink into Abhimanyu. He stayed quiet and allowed Abhimanyu to gravitate.

'You should know the MARCOS have arrived, and I've already briefed them. They're giving the army commandos a hard time.'

The MARCOS were revered not for no reason. Their regimen was a tough act to follow, and many army commandos took time to get used to it. Not surprisingly then, it was common for them to complain.

'Yes, I got a message from the Northeast Army Commander. You know how it is. I assured him his boys are doing great.' Amjad needed to role his dice to entice Abhimanyu. 'We have only one priority now. Find the mole who has been hiding amongst us for such a long time that we need a plan to flush him out of his hole.'

'What do you have in mind?'

The mole had shown his immaculate professional skills. He may not be tech savvy, but he knew his way to the right place at the right time. Despite the heavy security around the hard disk, he had gained access to it. He also managed to plant evidence to make IB chase ghosts of Pasha and got the Indians to kill an Indian informant. It wouldn't be easy for Amjad. The mole had proven his skillset, and they needed to beat him at his own game. They needed to be quick and sharp. Amjad needed a place to start.

'What if we send an advisory on a possible mole to limited people? If everyone is alert, someone might notice something,' Sonia wondered.

'The mole is industrious. What if he gets his hands on it? The mole will not only go quiet but will also know we are after him. We'll lose him forever.'

'What if we run a covert private investigation instead?'

'Privately within our own agencies? Can we do that?' Sonia was surprised.

'We've done it in the past. We can do it again. It'll just be a little more, should I say, risky to your career.' Amjad would need NSA's permission to do it, but they would still be on their own. If it went wrong, the agency wouldn't pick up the tab till they run the whole course of investigation. But desperate times call for desperate measures. Somewhere toward the end, the NSA would intervene and pull them out on classified grounds. It had happened in the past; it could be tried again.

'The hard disk was tagged the whole time,' Sonia murmured then continued with excitement. 'The logs of people who had access to the hard disk or the room where it was kept since it arrived.'

Amjad added, 'The evidence room log will not be comprehensive, but the list of people who have access will be limited and shouldn't be very long. We can profile them—their background, recent movements, foreign travel, changes in bank balances etc. It shouldn't take you more than a day, Sonia, right?'

'Absolutely.' Her voice was confident again.

'Say we have our suspects. The next question is how do we zero in on *the* one?'

They thought for some time, then Abhimanyu devised the classic bait technique. 'Send a direct mail or message saying we know about him. Hopefully, it disturbs them, and we catch the signs early enough.'

'We'll need to have a tail on all of them,' Amjad added.

'And we need to make sure they really feel we know it. If he is as smart as what we think, it'll be difficult to force him do something incriminating. The bait has to be convincing,' Abhimanyu said.

'Go on.' Amjad felt they were getting somewhere.

'We need him to be desperate, to make him contact the handler. That will be enough.'

It finally struck Amjad that could be the key. Abhimanyu was right. A handler was an informants' Achilles heel. 'Even if he sends a message to his handler and the recipient is a confirmed enemy, our job is done. We can incriminate him in the courts.' Amjad would need a few on-ground resources to tail the suspects simultaneously—sleeper cells unaware of each other's operations. It was beyond his remit, but he had thought of a solution.

'So, why don't you book me on the next flight then?'

Amjad smiled, for he had lured Abhimanyu in without even a bait.

IB Headquarters, January 23

The last four days hadn't been easy, but Amjad had managed to arrange many pieces. 'Finally, you've arrived.'

'Was always just a call away.'

'Hundred percent fit?'

'Does it matter?'

Amjad was right in his assessment; Abhimanyu wished retirement, but his heart still enjoyed the thrill of a mission. 'Didn't I tell you that you can't control your commando instincts?' The remark came loaded with a hope to motivate Abhimanyu, make him reconsider his premature retirement. A soldier like him was a priceless asset for any nation.

Abhimanyu got the whiff and chose not to respond—an uncharacteristic behavior of Abhimanyu, an unfortunate outcome for Amjad.

'There you are.' Sonia joined them, glad to see Abhimanyu back again. 'Don't grant him a leave next time.'

'If he takes my permission.' Amjad shrugged.

They followed Sonia's cue and walked with her to the cyber cell's war room.

'There is good news and bad news.'

'Like always,' Amjad remarked.

'Intelligence inputs from Zahir and IB were correct. Khalid's voice samples, fingerprints, and retina matched the encryption. We needed the binary DNA sequencing, but we are into the hard disk. Many of the files have been deleted, however about half the data is still there.'

'Any way to put together the lost data?'

'The only way, a very tedious one, is to triangulate all the data from all other databases across all intelligence teams in the country.'

'We've already found multiple aliases, running sleeper cells which have come alive in last three years.'

'Three years ago,' Abhimanyu thought out loud, 'we had the Chennai attack.'

'They've been planning this activity since they failed in Chennai. The disk has their pseudo names, contact information, including email addresses, even phone numbers. We've already found and tagged most of them. In some cases, most of their handlers are also in the Pakistani Embassy. In all, we've tagged thirty-five people across India.'

Abhimanyu and Amjad were in shock. It was not just one mole but a network of informants.

Sonia flicked through the photos on screen. 'IT engineers working in national information center, IPS Officers, doctors working in military hospitals, and even junior officers in the police. We can arrest all of them on a moment's notice, but the timing has to be managed.'

'What's the bad news?'

Sonia was quiet to collect her thoughts. 'The file on the disk has a folder named Cortex.'

That was a solid lead. Abhimanyu wondered what there was to be so afraid about; after all, they had been chasing for a lead all this while.

'After triangulating the information in the hard disk with other databases, we've mapped out their key activities. Their plan has five moving parts. For each part, there is a sleeper cell. The five parts include bringing in the fedayeen, setting them up with the documents, acclimatizing them, getting them resources and, lastly, setting them loose to complete the mission.'

Abhimanyu knew tracking the resources was the best way to follow their trail. The resources used in such missions were rare and always left a trail. 'What kind of resources are we talking about here?'

'Guns, bullets, vehicles, access cards, special meals etc.—supplies to hold out alone for a long time.' The trail had to be something else, something deadlier and more specific.

'Modus operandi?'

'It's a chain model. Sleeper cells are activated, they do their part, return to hibernation, and the next team takes over. Even if we directly intercept them, we'd only uncover a part of the chain at any stage. The larger network stays protected.'

'They simply outsource that activity to another cell and the mission is on.' Abhimanyu could see where Sonia was going.

'Exactly. And we can't wait for the whole event to play out either.'

Abhimanyu fathomed the sleeper cells would also have some sort of time constraint. 'Do we have a sense of timeline?'

Sonia cleared her throat. 'Yes. And that's the bad news. We mapped out the dates in the disk with a few guesses, the dates when each of these modules are active. We understand the first four modules are already back in hibernation. That means the fifth module is already active. They are in their last lap. The last module has been let loose to deliver the broken arrow.'

The news was not a surprise to Abhimanyu, but a confirmation of the doomsday scenario wasn't a lead to rejoice either. The lead had been extracted and unlocked, but it had also led them to a place they had hoped didn't exist—a place of no return. It was here and now. Even an accidental nuclear blast would escalate into a nuclear war, and at least half of the subcontinent would vanish within an hour.

'The nuke will go off in Assam on January twenty-sixth, oh-nine—India's Republic day.' Sonia's words gave despair a seat in the room. It was no longer concealed but very much visible and recognizable in everyone's eyes. In this game of chess, they had been put into checkmate. Forty-eight hours were not enough to make another move, and it would be a race against time just to save the day now.

Akram realized brooding over lack of time would not help, so he shifted gears and thought more like a soldier and less like a spy. Think straight, he told himself. They had to do what they had to do. First step was to locate the fedayeen before the time ran out on them. Intercepting and neutralizing them was the only task that could ensure the nukes didn't detonate.

Akram saw Abhimanyu was lost in his thoughts, perhaps worried about Sasha who was still in the Northeast. He intervened to break his thoughts. 'We have forty-eight hours. Let's use it.'

Abhimanyu, back to his senses, nodded and turned to Sonia. 'Let's go through everything. Tell us everything you have found about their operation.'

Sonia put up the map of the infiltration route. 'A three-member team infiltrated India a month ago through Gilgit in Kashmir. A sleeper cell called Shaheen was deputed to help them in crossing the border.'

'Do we know them?'

Sonia toggled to the data from the hard disk. 'Yes. Two members of Shaheen work in a tea stall outside the Shopian Police Station, one in an Anantnag Post Office, one in a Baramulla bus station office, and one in the Kargil Police Station.'

'Anything from government records?'

'Yes, and it all adds up. The men in Anantnag and Baramula were on privilege leave together. The one at the Baramula Police Station, Abdullah Salim, also applied for sick leave on the same days, so all of them were out on the same dates.'

'How long back was this?'

'Two years! On January tenth, oh-seven.'

It was a moment of reckoning for Amjad. He realized they were up against a meticulously planned attack and they had only been playing catchup since 2007. How deep was their planning, and how could the Indians get ahead of them for once? The answers eluded him. 'How did you track two years old government records?'

'We didn't. We just went by the information on the hard disk. It had a call scheduled to this sleeper cell,

Shaheen, on December first, oh-six, and there was no mention of this till January first, and guess what?'

'The documentation cells?'

'Absolutely. A person in Delhi's Chandni Chowk was contacted. He makes fake driving licenses and passports. The local police has arrested him a couple of times, but each time, his political sources got him out on bail.'

'Who is that source?' Akram asked in frustration.

'Anand Kabadiwala, member of parliament. He has built a business empire around illegal papers in Chandni Chowk. Not surprisingly, many cases have been brought against his party men for aiding forgery but to no avail.'

'Talk about selling out your country, and he is in the parliament!' Effectively, the parliamentarians' illegal side business had cost them two years of precious time.

'Hey, we're working for the one billion Indians.' Amjad got them some perspective. It was futile to entertain any additional negativity.

'Most aliases in the documentation cell have a connection with Anand Kabadiwala. As one would expect, this sleeper cell went inactive after a month.'

'Where are they now?'

'They are through the chain—'

'On their way to plant the broken arrow in Assam. We're still mapping their rout, but someone, a detonator, a key person in the chain already awaits them in Assam. This person's identity is unknown. The disk just refers to him as A2111.' Sonia handed them the files. A2111 appeared many times. The team had deduced him to be some sort of a failsafe check on the mission because the broken arrow's lock was mapped to the detonator's fingerprint. The detonator was the most important person of the mission. It would be impossible to find someone hidden in the jungles of Assam in less than forty-eight hours.

'It's too late to find this person now.'

Abhimanyu agreed and nodded.

'Tell me more about the detonator.' Amjad was still stuck on it.

'The detonator is linked to Azghar because his reference comes up almost in every document alongside Azghar. The frequency of references suggest he has been a part of the plot since the very beginning and in India for a long time. It's surprising that we have no trace of him.' Sonia had crosschecked the phone numbers, the email addresses, and even the location references for this person, but nothing matched anything in the internal records.

Amjad guessed the detonator to be, most likely, one of Azghar's close aides or a youth raised by Azghar himself or his men. The detonator belonged to the inner circle. They had come across a similar individual, Zowoski

Kiraja, who had turned out to be a relative of an Evil Seven member. The Indians had him in custody now.

'The detonator's a dead-end. We better find the three fedayeen. They're our best bet,' Akram reiterated.

This time Amjad chose to keep quiet.

'What do you have on the three-member team?' Abhimanyu asked.

'A lot more. A certain Rupesh Khamba, an ex-Indian Army commando, leads this team. He went missing after a court martial found him guilty of taking bribes from terrorists to release some of them in the guise of an ambush. We think the very same terrorist organization recruited him for Cortex soon after the court martial. References on the hard disk tag him to the same Lashkar.'

'Family?'

'None. No liabilities. Money is the main driver. A ten million dollar transfer against his bank account in Mauritius is recorded in the hard disk.' That was enough to incriminate him but they needed more than that now.

'What about the other two?'

'Czech-based Akhlaq and Iran-based Jahangir are his helpers.' She toggled to their photos. 'They've been active in Syria while transporting fissile material across North Korea and Pakistan for at least the last decade or so.' Sonia toggled back to the fedayeen's route. 'Based on our chronology of events, they should be somewhere in Assam already.'

Amjad studied the map and rushed to the nearest desktop. It was uncharacteristic of him, but it was clear he had chanced upon something. He logged into his account. Amjad opened the daily review file from his mail. *Suspicious movement reported in Sandakphu national park.* 'The local army intelligence spotted it, and it came up in my daily dossier. I thought it must be the deed of notorious smugglers, but its huge size still intrigued me. So I had it tagged anyway.' Amjad called the IB Chief, Prem Galwaokar, who was in Delhi market lanes on a mission. 'The tag in Assam …'

'Yes, what about it?'

'It's hot.'

Prem got off the market lane and found a place where he was alone. 'The wildlife and thick forest cover is making our lives difficult, but we have activated our local intelligence network. There are a couple of photos.' Prem covered his head with a towel. The IB Chief couldn't be seen in the Delhi locales in such shabby clothes. The IB Chief forwarded a mail from his pad to Amjad. 'Some big vehicles, unusual on those roads.'

Amjad projected it on the screen, and Sonia recognized it at the first glance. 'It's an armored vehicle, similar to the one described in the disk.' A miniaturized nuke was three to four tons in weight, and with the support equipment would weigh seven to eight tons. Sonia deduced, a ten-tonner was an ideal size.

Amjad traced the coordinates on the map where the IB sleuths had spotted the ten-tonner. The truck had consistently been moving eastward. 'They're headed to Guwahati.' It was the largest Indian city in the Northeast.

A gloomy silence befell the room, for a city of a million Indians was about to be reduced to a rubble.

Amjad sensed the mood and stood to calm their nerves. 'For the first time in this mission, we are ahead of them. They'll take another day to drive to Guwahati. We can intercept them well before they reach Guwahati.' Abhimanyu knew the next challenge. 'It'll be a disaster even if they accidentally detonate it. We must intercept them without giving them a chance to detonate it, like Chennai.'

'Kill them before they realize we're on to them and diffuse the nuke. If we can't, we airlift it to the bay,' Akram added.

Sonia's team had put them ahead, but it would only hold on for a while.

'It's a go,' Amjad said without batting an eyelid.

Amidst all of it, they still had no idea where the detonator would actually meet them. They had to act before they lost the edge, before the detonator met the terrorists.

Abhimanyu eyed the IB Chief, Prem. 'We're flying to Guwahati. Assuming we have the truck's coordinates by the time we land in Guwahati, we'll need an MI-35 M-class to intercept them.' The M-class was fitted with powerful noise silencers and advanced avionics, adept for discreet night missions. Abhimanyu knew each of them inside out. 'I'll need the copter number eleven of Agni Squadron. '

The IB Chief had heard about Abhimanyu's penchant for flying but was still pleasantly surprised at the specificity of his request. He regarded Amjad; the chief was impressed.

Abhimanyu had been trained on many skills, and knowing all the details of every equipment he had ever operated was one of them, as it was for all MARCOS. He was still special. Abhimanyu had seen the specs of this particular copter in one of his flying classes a year back and recalled, rightly, it was stationed in the Indian Army's Tezpur Base, not far from Guwahati.

Amjad dialed Colonel Shahid. 'We can't risk the cannon guns on a nuclear truck, so we'll also need low-altitude heavy lux shooting capability to blind them out. Just a minor modification, your engineers should be able to do it before we land in Guwahati.'

'Right on it. My men will tune up the things just like you've always wanted it.'

Abhimanyu was a well-known helicopter pilot across services. He was amongst the few pilots whose weapon choices were documented for training purposes. He had trained with Colonel Shahid, who counted Abhimanyu as his best recruit. By Colonel's own judgement, Abhimanyu had the capability to surpass him in copter maneuvering skills.

All of them were more settled, except Sonia, who was eager to share something more. 'There is one more thing.'

Amjad refocused on her screen.

'We have more than one nuke,' Sonia quipped. Her words caused an indelible expression on all their faces.

'What do you mean?' Abhimanyu asked.

'While we could only trace one detonator, there are two nuke instances. The detonator's file also has references to two assault teams, AT01 and AT02. No other details are available. No one is infiltrating it, no one is carrying it, and no one is responsible for it. It only appears as another instance in some of the files with Cortex tagged to it.'

'Anything on the location?'

'There are many instances of joint work between AT01 and AT02, but the trail on AT02 disappears beyond that. So, all we can say is it's also in the Northeast.' Amjad eyed Prem in despair.

'Perhaps it was a part of the deleted files. Perhaps another similar hard disk exists, a similar cell. We don't know anything about it. Which is why it's more dangerous,' Abhimanyu answered.

'The detonator is the key. There is only one detonator, and the truck can lead us to the detonator, and the detonator can lead us to the other nuke.' Prem was right. That connect was the next best thing to a concrete lead they had.

Abhimanyu immediately agreed to the plan. 'Keep commando teams and bomb diffusion squads on standby. Moment you have anything on the detonator or the other nuke, we'll be ready to make our move.' For Abhimanyu, it was time to hit the roads again.

'All roads lead to Guwahati,' Amjad concluded, and the MARCOS signed off from the cyber cell room.

The IL-76 spread its wings at Delhi's Palam Airport with MARCOS in its belly to begin the final sequence.

Guwahati Airport

It was three days to India's Republic Day, and the night was just beginning to take hold. Emergency protocols were activated, and the MARCOS landed at the Guwahati Airport midst pitch darkness guided largely by the aircraft instrument systems. The airport was practicing wartime protocols. Major General Arup Kannan, head of IB's Eastern command, was ready to set them up for their next step basis the brief from the headquarters. 'The helicopter is ready. MI-35M.' It was locked and loaded, ready on the tarmac. 'A team of four commandos will accompany you. They're the best from Army's Eastern command.' Arup handed him their coordinates. 'Feed them into your pads. Our rangers have scouted them. They are still in the jungle roads.'

'Time to hit them?'

'Difficult to predict exactly. They're moving eastward on NH-31. Our satellites are following them, but the green cover and the terrain isn't helping. The Space Research wing is ensuring we triangulate enough data not to lose them, and the exact time to reach them will depend on their moves. Your helicopter has a direct feed, and we will be in touch to communicate on that.'

Abhimanyu gave the major general a firm handshake. 'Keep your men on alert. We're not chasing a ghost this time.'

Sonia's deductions were clear, and Abhimanyu was sure it was now or never. 'It won't be easy to hide a ten-ton nuke on these roads.'

'No. But it will be naïve to expect they don't have a rabbit up their sleeve,' Abhimanyu interrupted.

Major General Arup thought it unlikely but wondered how much he didn't know.

'In that case, we'll need to scan the whole Northeast. The mountains, the forests, the rivers, and borders on all sides make it impossible. China, Bangladesh, and even Myanmar have breached those mountains from all sides in the past.' Arup was overwhelmed at even the thought.

'That's why we need a lead on the second nuke, and you need to keep your resources on it.' Abhimanyu was right; their approach had to be laser sharp.

Major General nodded. 'But how?'

'We need to be there when they make their first mistake. They'll have to come out of their den at some point to complete their mission. That's our moment. The satellites, drones, local intelligence—all the assets should report every suspicious movement no matter how small. While we go after the first broken arrow, the other one has to be pursued equally aggressively.'

They walked toward the helicopter.

'Connect with Sonia in Delhi. She'll get you all the information you'll need on someone we just call the detonator. You'll understand what I mean.'

General Arup finally agreed with Abhimanyu's analysis. 'You could be right, and I understand that's the best guess we have. My boys will be on it, Abhimanyu, even though I pray we're wrong. I pray there is no other nuke.' Arup smiled and waved. 'See you on the other side soon.'

'See you, General.' Abhimanyu boarded the helicopter, switched on the rotors, did the regular flight check and flew toward his next destination—NH 31.

CHAPTER 16

CALAMITY ON WHEELS

Northeast India

It was more than sixteen hours since Akhlaq had been driving, but he didn't feel drowsy yet. Sleep had deserted him; he was high on adrenaline. Revenge seethed in his eyes. Its fury was enough to burn down the city beyond the jungles to ashes. Akhlaq was on a holy mission he had prepared for as long as he could remember. Infidels had killed his parents when he was a toddler. The memory of the night when Russian forces had executed mass bombings in his hometown in Afghanistan still haunted him. He had only been two years old, but he could vividly recall the incident. A seething desire of revenge had burned in him ever since. Azghar had spotted the scar and knew his fire would turn him into a great asset, so he enrolled Akhlaq in a secret camp operated by the Afghanistan's rebel forces.

Young recruits from all over the world were taught the tenets of sacrifice here. Sacrifice was the only form of worship that would get them freedom from the eternal pain. Their souls would heal, and they would emerge on the other side cleansed of all sins. Akhlaq's commitment had inspired many local rebels, and he was already a celebrated figure in his camp. He viewed western-style political systems and democracies as an enemy—the non-believers, Satan. What better way to attain freedom from eternal pain than to kill a million infidels. His regularity with the rituals and ruthlessness in the field had helped him gain trust of the top commanders. Eventually, they had entrusted him with facilitating the holiest of all missions—a nuclear fedayeen mission. Akhlaq was driving toward his ultimate destination, and his eyes wanted to soak up every sight tonight.

Jahangir woke to take over from Akhlaq. He knew Akhlaq's mind and body needed rest. Jahangir was his senior and understood the importance of being fully alert when they hit the city. They were still twelve hours from the city of a million people, and a million things could go wrong in these moments. He eyed Rupesh—just an infidel who sold his soul to betray his own kind. Such men had only one religion: money. Rupesh had managed to get them across the Nepal border, and so, he would be paid the pending half of his money duly. He was a relaxed man and had gone to sleep a few minutes ago soon after they had crossed the Nepal border. They needed such infidels for a successful mission. The seniors had said to obey him, for he knew the roads and had the contacts. So, they tolerated Rupesh's commands. Once they reached the city, they were scheduled to stop at the drop point where the infidel would leave them for good. From thereon, it was up to Jahangir and Akhlaq to finish the mission. Money would go to Rupesh, but the real reward was reserved for Jahangir and Akhlaq. Heaven awaited them. The gods would pay them well. A good deal to have any day.

The satellite phone beeped, interrupting Jahangir's thoughts. It wasn't supposed to beep. He was extremely surprised. The instructions were as clear as possible. There was no need of any last moment communication. However, only his masters had the phone link, and if they had decided to call, it must have been something urgent, so he asked Akhlaq to stop the truck. Jahangir walked away from Rupesh, for he didn't trust an infidel, even in his sleep.

The dark roads disappeared into the night as he walked away from the headlights and stopped fifty meters ahead in the middle of the jungle.

'Aslaam Valikum,' a soft voice said on the other side, and it didn't take Jahangir long to recognize it.

Out of respect, he went onto his knees. 'Aaleyah, I am blessed to hear your voice. Allah must be very happy with me. No better time to hear your voice than just before our martyrdom.' After taking the blessings, Jahangir stood and listened carefully. Surprise had turned into shock, but it was Aaleyah's command, and he had to abide by it at any cost. 'I will do everything just as you say, Aaleyah. Our martyrdom will not be wasted.'

The phone disconnected from other side.

Jahangir looked skyward and closed his eyes, for the Gods had invited him before the scheduled time. Jahangir slid into the truck cabin. 'Turn around. We have to change course.'

Confused, Akhlaq leaned into his ears, careful of the infidel beside them. 'Are we abandoning the mission? I can't. I have to finish what I came for.'

'No, idiot. We are preponing it.'

Akhlaq felt fear then elation. 'But what about him?'

'He goes with us,' Jahangir replied with one finger on his lips.

Akhlaq's happiness knew no bounds. The infidels' commands had pestered him all along the trip. There was no better revenge than to kill him alongside them. Of course, he won't get to Heaven, for he hadn't made any holy sacrifices. He was just a money whore.

Guwahati Command Center

The army couldn't do it alone. Major General Arup knew it very well. He needed every help he could get; an integrated response to track and diffuse the broken arrow was the need of the hour. And the only way to ensure perfect coordination was to get the chiefs together. As the general in the field, his powers superseded hierarchy now. It was his moment to shine. 'Get me the headquarters online. IB, ISRO, and RAW.'

Amjad straightened his collar. Not often did he interact with his direct boss—the RAW Chief Rajnish Gogoi. The RAW Chief was known to wander in the obscurity, away from the public glare. It took the operator less than ten minutes to say, 'We have them online, sir.' Today, even Ranjan Gogoi had to surface.

Arup cleared his throat to brief the chiefs. 'Sir, intelligence has confirmed a terrorist module is out to detonate a broken arrow in the Northeast. We are tracking everything that resembles our leads on the nuke-mounted truck. Guwahati seems to be the target for now.'

The IB Chief, Prem, and RAW Chief Ranjan were quiet. The only chief in genuine shock was the ISRO head. 'Is it a drill?' he asked innocently, for he was the only one completely clueless.

'No, sir. This is as real as it feels. I request your best brains onto this, men you would trust with your life. Also, we can't risk any leak, any paranoia, or any incompetence.' The ISRO Chief was naïve but a sensible man. He was terrified but knew it was the right time to call in the cavalry, more than ever.

'Get me all the team leads from the intelligence wing on line two,' ISRO's Chief instructed his executive assistant. Intelligence wing was the classified team in ISRO that used all the available ISRO technologies to scan, detect, and feed information for the hunters.

Each team leader had an area of expertise, like thermal scanning, pixel zooming, terrain mapping, remote sensing, imaging, and many others. They needed it all.

They not just needed to scan the entire East in only a few hours but also had to guide the commandos to the bomb's location and diffuse it. The point wasn't lost on Rajnish. 'Any leads on the bomb location or any movement?'

Arup looked at Sonia for the latest information.

'There is a decoy plan certainly, but we havn't detected any suspicious movement yet. One can guess that it could have been transported already.' Sonia's deduction was logical and frightening. 'A miniaturized nuke can be put in a passive state and activated at the right time. However, it's not possible to move it around much without a very high risk of explosion. It implies that the nuke must be put close to its target, so our area of scanning remains the same—all the major cities and their immediate outskirts, areas which are close enough to the city but far enough for storage.' After some thought, she continued, 'We should dedicate all the spare resource bandwidth to survey the incoming and outgoing roads across all the major cities in East India, also near all major border checkpoints. Those are the two spots they'll have to compulsorily cross.'

'What about mountains, forests, and national parks?' The ISRO Chief was getting overwhelmed. He had no time to recce twice.

'Well, if they are in the mountains and forests, the danger to human life is minimal. We don't have time to look for them there, and we don't need to look everywhere. We need to rank their possible targets, which is a tall task.' Sonia's strategic acumen was not lost on the chiefs.

Though they were constrained by resources and time, they had a field sense of the task ahead. The hard disk had given them an edge. The chiefs then realized they were ahead of the terrorists who still did not know the Indians were coming for them. The Indians had to make it count. If there would ever be any mission that would exemplify the best of all these services, it was here.

Major General Arup broke the contemplative silence across the room. 'In Chennai, we barely had any leads, but we came out on top. The odds don't matter now. The only thing that counts is the result.'

The chiefs nodded in unison.

Amjad was happy to see the three chiefs coming together. The service had to often work at odds with each other. Bureaucratic walls and political interference often meant that for any extra budget, they had to gain an edge over the other in the eyes of the Indian bureaucracy and the government. After all, the government had to divide the same pie between all of them. Add to that the political stooges nurtured by every power center in parliament. The interference was often debilitating. The structures, often weak. However, for seventy years since India's independence, in times like these, individual patriotism outmatched institutional failures. Only time would tell if it will be enough. The three chiefs had their heart set on the field action. They prepared for an intense battle of intelligence.

Amjad checked the time. 'Get me Alpha, India online.'

Arup dialed in and waited a few seconds. 'Alpha, India, come in with your location.' He would repeat at the same pace till there was an echo.

'ETA, five minutes. Teesta River in sight. Prepare to force stop on bridge number forty-nine.' Abhimanyu knew they would have limited options to escape from the bridge.

'Can we get the truck on screen as well?'

Meanwhile, General Arup and Amjad were perplexed to see the truck turning around.

'They've changed course. They're no longer coming toward Guwahati. They're moving back.'

Everyone had the same question; what had prompted them to turn around, or was it just a diversion?

Sonia traced back the truck's route. 'They had turned around about the same time you took off.'

Tension was in the air, and every bone could feel the chill. Stress was scripted across their faces. Amjad and Abhimanyu had the same thought now.

Amjad searched for anyone who had made a recent entry or exit. He tried to read the faces in the room, but none seemed suspect. Everyone in the room was genuinely concerned. 'General,' Amjad whispered into General Arup's ears, 'do you trust your people with your life?'

'Every one of them.' His voice was stern. 'But something has surely ticked them off.'

They checked the satellite's live feed. Each pixel accounted for a meter, and at such sharpness, it was hard to interpret the on-ground movement. The ISRO team connected the incoming stream into their video grab software, which enhanced the video quality to o.1 meter. The enhanced video came onto the screen, and a gloom descended upon the room.

'It is indeed the miniaturized nuke.' Amjad could see the terrorists working on the bomb. 'What are they doing?'

'Activating it,' Sonia said in a low voice.

Abhimanyu wondered if it could get any worse from here.

'Even if it does not blast, it will lead to massive radiation leaks,' someone said.

'How do we know if it's active?' Abhimanyu asked, yet hopeful.

'As soon as they came out and opened the trunk, the radiations spiked on our trackers. It was in passive state till now. It's definitely active now.'

Amjad gathered his senses, realizing there was no time to waste, and eyed Sonia. 'They were going southwest from the Namchi bypass, which leads to Guwahati. They have now turned south from Namchi, which will … lead them to Siliguri. That's their target now.'

'So, we need to stop them before they reach Siliguri and also prevent any radiation leaks?' Abhimanyu was ruffled but tried to sound calm.

'Yes,' Sonia said.

After a brief pause, Abhimanyu had decided. 'So be it. Can you give me visuals on the monitors here?'

'Ahh … sure. You should have it …. now.'

The satellites tracking the ten-tonner streamed directly on Abhimanyu's monitor in the copter. The recently installed touchscreens gave him access to the satellite feeds, which he had already mastered over the years. The only downside was many of the flight metrics normally available on the monitor would not be visible now. Abhimanyu had to shift to manual mode and rely only on his instincts now. 'They will still cross Teesta Bridge in about thirty minutes. General, tell me, your commandos don't swim by any chance?'

'That's why we've got the MARCOS.' It was a no. 'Though they can take down the bridge and level the river for you.'

'Fair enough.' Abhimanyu laughed and regarded the commandos, who gave him a thumbs up. Each commando force had a unique skillset, and Abhimanyu respected it.

They had solved one problem but would have to manage a bigger one soon. The truck had change course, and if it was due to a mole, then Abhimanyu had to cut that off immediately, so he decided to cut off all feeds, including the GPS, except the incoming satellite feed. It was a risky gamble in case something were to happen to the helicopter, but he had to protect his location and movements at all costs. The mole, no matter how smart, couldn't use an incoming satellite feed either, and that was all Abhimanyu needed.

Watching the truck, he announced his intentions. 'We are going offline.'

'What-What are you doing? We need to have eyes on the ground!' Arup was befuddled.

'I don't trust any of those eyes now, General.'

Amjad put his hands around Arup's shoulder to calm him down. 'That's okay.' He would have done the same had he been in Abhimanyu's place. He would have trusted his own instincts and only his own men. It was the best way to plug a leak.

The copter went offline, the screens went blank, and Sonia switched off the satellite feeds. Abhimanyu and Sonia, two MARCOS between them, had blacked out the entire setup of Indian intelligence. They were free to do it in their own way now, and no one could do anything except wait for Abhimanyu's next communication.

In the air, Abhimanyu realized his earphones contained signal disturbance even after switching off all the feeds. The earphones, specially designed by DRDO to detect any unusual disturbance, couldn't be wrong. In the manual mode, it should have gone silent, but it hadn't, which only meant one thing; the helicopter was compromised. A device, a tracker of some sort, was still inside the helicopter, perhaps emitting a signal at an unknown frequency. Abhimanyu immediately activated the kill-switch designed to ensure the helicopter blocked any outgoing signal on all frequencies. The disturbance stopped immediately. There was indeed a device. Someone had planted a tracker, compromising the helicopter. That's how they knew their locations, and that's why the truck drivers had changed their route. The mole proved resourceful, but it was no more a surprise for Abhimanyu. He felt ready for him. Bring it on, he said to himself then faced Akram. 'The copter was compromised.'

Akram looked across the valley into the pitch-dark horizon with a smile. 'The army has been compromised, but they don't know; we know. And we are out of grid.' Akram plotted the truck's route on the monitor to plan the best approach. 'The south end of the Teesta River, twenty minutes from here. That's where we set the trap.'

'They'll die in Teesta either way,' Abhimanyu said scornfully and lowered his helicopter to maintain low altitude.

Twenty minutes later, army commandos took position behind the trees. They were on time and ready with their setup. A white spot emerged on their rifles' scope. It grew bigger rather quickly. Soon, as it turned at the horizon, they could see it completely. The vehicle looked like a beast, running on sixteen tires and carrying nothing less than ten tons. The truck approached them at sixty kilometers per hour, faster than they had anticipated. One wrong move and no one would be alive to tell the tale of how they had stopped the calamity on wheels.

'Three men in front,' the first commando, a spotter, said into the earbuds.

'Rupesh, Jahangir, and Akhlaq.' Siddhartha identified them from his vantage on top of a tree on other side of the bridge. His scope reconfirmed their identities.

'They're coming right at us, sir. Should I shoot?' the commando asked with an anxious voice and nervous hands. No one was trained well to shoot at a nuclear truck.

'No. Let them enter the bridge.'

'We're losing the angle,' the commando said as the truck approached the bridge.

'No shootings. Hold your fingers as much as you can. Block it as soon as they enter. Our best-case scenario is for them to surrender,' Abhimanyu said. It was an unlikely event but was worth a try.

'This may not go the best way.' Even Akram was nervous. He didn't expect the terrorists to hesitate in pulling the trigger.

'This will go exactly that way.' Abhimanyu removed a device from a case Dr. Manish Chelliyappam had given him.

'A phone?'

'No.' It was time to put those gadgets to use. Even as Abhimanyu's hand steered the helicopter, his focus was on the monitor. The truck was entering the bridge.

'This is coming your way, Abhimanyu.'

Abhimanyu zoomed in on the monitors to see they were wearing suicide vests. 'No, I have a feeling this is coming your way. They're wearing their vests. Siddhartha, keep your scopes on them.' Abhimanyu pulled up the jockey as he emerged from under the bridge.

Siddhartha's palms were wet, for he had a nuclear target on his scope.

Akram and Siddhartha couldn't believe it, but they had heard a lot about Abhimanyu's flying capabilities. It inspired confidence. At least someone knew what he was doing.

Abhimanyu kept the helicopter hovering below the bridge, waiting for the right moment. As the truck approached the middle of the bridge, he swung away his helicopter from under the bridge and swung it back on top of the bridge then hovered right in front of the truck—a shock and awe tactic. The timing had to be precise, giving them just enough opportunity to slow the truck but not long enough for the truck driver to make a move. Abhimanyu saw Rupesh straight in his eyes. Rupesh wasn't a stranger to Abhimanyu. Abhimanyu had seen him on trial and had read about his subsequent disappearance. It felt odd to have his own countryman on the other side of this nuclear attack, but so was the world around him—untrustworthy and unreliable.

Rupesh smiled back at him and produced a light machinegun.

Jahangir slammed the truck into Reverse as Rupesh fired firing at the helicopter.

Abhimanyu shouted through the mic, 'Blow it off, now!'

Commandos blew off the trees and blocked the bridge at both ends.

Seeing the trees fall, Jahangir instinctively pressed the brake pedal. There was no point in ramming it into the trees with an active nuke in the truck. The nuke was meant for the millions of infidels; this was a place in the middle of nowhere and not the way he had dreamt of sacrificing his life. He decided to change the gears, but Abhimanyu had activated blindingly bright lights fixed on the nose of the helicopter and focused it on the truck cabin. The lux levels were so high that even the commandos at the other end had to cover their eyes with both hands. All three terrorists were completely blinded.

Abhimanyu landed the chopper on the bridge, and two army commandos rushed out with guns forward.

Knees bent, they carefully approached the truck while Siddhartha gave them the cover from his perch on the tree.

The terrorists had ducked below the screen.

Abhimanyu said into the amplifier, 'You can't escape. You either surrender or we shoot you.'

Rupesh got down with Jahangir and Akhlaq who were wearing suicide jackets. Rupesh didn't have one, but he realized the commandos would hesitate to shoot at him in case they thought he did.

Akhlaq was visibly frustrated at being pinned down. It was make or break for him. The detonator was not there, but, if he managed to blast his vest in the trunk, maybe the bomb would explode, so he dashed for the trunk and ran around the truck's right side, for it was hidden from the helicopter—but not from Siddhartha.

He had him in the open from his perch down the bridge and wasted no time taking him out. Two head shots in a moment ensured Akhlaq didn't have any time to reach the trunk. Abhimanyu removed a pad device and pointed it at Jahangir. It seemed like a blast of wave, perhaps EMP, because it soon short-circuited the truck's electronics.

Rupesh and Jahangir were disoriented. It was one of Mac's latest designs yet to be field tested, but Mac said it would work. If the suicide vest was one of the regular ones, it would have been neutralized. It was indeed a regular one. Jahangir felt a few sparks in his vest. Something had gone wrong. He immediately tried to detonate it but couldn't.

'So, this works. Good job, Mac,' Abhimanyu muttered to himself.

The commandos reached the truck. 'Hands behind your back! Get to the side!' they repeated.

The terrorists looked just as nervous as the commandos now.

'Remove the life jackets!' Abhimanyu shouted.

'Same old, same old. If I'm not wrong, you are Abhimanyu.'

The shock silenced him.

Reading the silence, Jahangir knew he was right. 'Your tricks won't stop us and our comrades! We will come for you!'

Rupesh raised one hand and rolled his other one in some sort of a signal. Jahangir and Rupesh ran toward the railing of the bridge.

'Don't move! Stop! Stop!' It was futile, but the commandos still shouted at them.

They were going to jump off the bridge, so the commandos took their shots. Rupesh was immediately hit in his leg, but he kept walking. Two more shots in his legs were needed to stop him. However, Jahangir managed to reach the railing and jump into the river. Rupesh laid on the ground, nursing his wounds and angry, for it meant he had just lost the millions promised to him. Now that the promise of millions was gone, his survival instincts kicked in. He quickly realized his chances to survive lay in him helping the Indians now. 'Bridge and trees worked in Pakistan, not again,' he said with a sly smile even though he grimaced from the pain in his bloodstained legs.

Abhimanyu realized he had been tagged, at least since the Kulnagar attack in Pakistan, and they knew his civilian identity.

Rupesh, for his part, had a new target now: Abhimanyu, the man who had robbed him of a million dollars. 'Jahangir will make sure we detonate the other device.'

Abhimanyu looked over the bridge. 'If he stays alive.'

An amphibious boat sped through the bridge with searchlights fitted at the bow and Akram at its helm. Another one emerged from the banks, captained by Siddhartha who had abandoned his position to join Akram in the third man's pursuit.

Jahangir had jumped from the bridge, hoping to flow downstream with the waters. Little did he know that two of the best navy divers were waiting for him. Jahangir noticed them and shuddered. 'Dadhiwali fauj,' he muttered to himself. The MARCOS had earned that nickname in Kashmir where they guarded the many rivers, ravines, and lakes. Jahangir realized immediately he had no chance of escaping.

Akram shot him in the leg as soon as he hit the waters and made a quick work of it. No one could swim without legs, upstream or downstream.

Siddhartha dove in to get Jahangir on their boat as Akram kept him firmly in the lights. He had failed his mission, and now he sat there, tied down in Siddhartha's boat instead of being at the gates of Heaven.

Akram regarded Abhimanyu with more respect. His idea to carry the inflatable boats had saved the day. They pulled Rupesh and Jahangir into the chopper and cuffed them. Siddhartha and Akram secured the bridge while the commandos took defensive positions.

Abhimanyu reactivated the communications and ran to the truck's trunk. 'AB01 is in sight. We have eyes on the nuke.'

The officers in the command center waited in suspense, focused on the screen, except Sonia. The screen was blank. She watched her monitor for any signals. As soon as she saw an incoming signal, she linked it to the screen.

'Where are the terrorists?' Amjad asked.

'One killed. Two captured.' Abhimanyu's voice broke the suspense.

The officers were elated and spontaneously burst into clapping. 'Bravo.' 'That's the way!'

Abhimanyu climbed into the trunk and checked the panels connected to the bomb.

Sonia could see them too now.

'Massive radiation spike,' Abhimanyu remarked as the readings on his hand pad went beyond critical levels.

'It's a nuke,' Sonia said.

The cheering stopped.

'The bomb disposal squad is already in the air, ETA thirty minutes. We still have a few hours on the timer here. We should manage to get it diffused in time,' Arup reassured Abhimanyu.

'It won't go off without the detonator's fingerprints anyway. But it's active, so be careful,' Amjad said and shifted gears. They needed more information on the second bomb; it was no time to quiz a hardened terrorist like Jahangir and lose time. Rupesh was their best bet.

Abhimanyu thought as much, rushed to the helicopter and studied Rupesh's weary eyes. He stepped on Rupesh's injured leg and pressed it hard enough for him to scream. There was no time to play games. 'Where is the second nuke?'

Rupesh was pleasantly surprised, for this could be his ticket to freedom. Jahangir and Akhlaq had never shared the details with him, but he had travelled together and knew enough to bail himself out. It was going to be a gameplay. 'Oh, you know about it?'

'Of course, we know about it. Now you'll spit out everything you know, or I'll shoot you right through your temple.'

Rupesh groaned from the pain but gathered himself quickly. 'What's in it for me?'

Abhimanyu was infuriated. The pain should have been enough.

'What do you need?' a voice asked from Abhimanyu's satellite phone.

Rupesh recognized that voice even on a satellite phone. 'Wow, is that you, Amjad? I heard you have grown and survived the agency politics well.' Amjad and Rupesh had a history. In fact, Amjad had played a critical role behind the scenes in collecting the evidence that had finally gotten Rupesh court martialed. Though the records were never made public, Rupesh knew the truth.

'What do you need?'

'It's only appropriate that you're the negotiator for my demands, you see. For only someone like you can achieve it, and, in my case, who better than you?'

'What do you need? You have a minute.'

'Oh, I have a lot of time. I know you don't have time, so let us keep it straight. I need a pardon, a complete pardon. Can you arrange that, Amjad?'

Amjad didn't like it, but Rupesh was a seasoned professional. Bargaining would prove futile, and they couldn't afford any delaying tactics. After a short moment of contemplation, Amjad agreed. 'We'll get it done for you, but you'll walk out only after you've shared credible information with us.'

Arup looked at Amjad, surprised. It was beyond their authority. Amjad wagged at him to trust his judgement.

'No, no … not going to fall for a verbal agreement. I know the system. Get me a presidential pardon.'

Amjad had his hands on his head. They couldn't fool around with Rupesh, for he knew the system too well for their liking. A presidential pardon had been arranged only once in history when a dreaded terrorist had to be exchanged in return for a few hijacked political families. The families were of utmost importance, and it went all the way to the top. The news was never released to the media, and no one knew about it except for the agency managing it. Amjad happened to be the security-in-charge on that exfiltration mission, and Rupesh had been a soldier on the same team. Both knew how it worked.

As per the set mechanism, only a handwritten letter of pardon signed by the President of India qualified. The letter, valid in all courts of India as per an article tugged in one of the anti-terrorist laws, never surfaced in public as the terrorists fled the country never to return. To keep it under wraps, it was in Indians' interest to let Rupesh disappear into oblivion. Rupesh knew exactly what he was talking about, and even Abhimanyu couldn't fathom Amjad's response.

With deep regret, Amjad decided to yield. 'I'll get it if your information turns out to be true. I'll need an hour after you tell us what you know. Deal?'

'First, the pardon letter delivered directly to my mail inbox.' Bruised and shot, his mind was still sharp. Rupesh knew his leverage would only last till he kept quiet. It couldn't be given away without a solid bargaining prize.

'Okay. I will be back.' Amjad excused himself.

Everyone in the room was left clueless. After all, he couldn't just call the president and ask him to sign a pardon letter for a terrorist who had just tried to nuke the country. Arup didn't believe Amjad would really try to pull it off.

Knowing him, Sonia had lesser doubts.

Abhimanyu had caught the drift by now as well. Even as the army helicopters covered the bridge and the commandos announced, 'Nukes secured,' Abhimanyu knew the night was still young. Rupesh's threat had a boast of genuine information. By far, that was their best lead on the second nuke and the reason they were, again, far behind the terrorists for now.

CHAPTER 17

PIN IN THE HAYSTACK

Teesta River, Sikkim

It didn't take Amjad an hour but just thirty minutes. 'We've mailed it to you, just like you asked. Now, tell us all you know.'

Rupesh eyed Abhimanyu, and he let him access his email on the pad. 'That's your ID.'

'You keep surprising me beyond measure.'

Rupesh removed a small, well-hidden device from the back of his buckle.

Abhimanyu was taken aback to realize it didn't show up in the body search. The cargos were well-padded and designed to hide such devices.

Rupesh checked for the email, sent it to a few aliases and pressed some buttons. The device self-destructed. Rupesh had run a shredder app which burnt and destroyed the tab disk as well as the processor. He had seen the pardon letter earlier, so he knew this was indeed an original. 'You've kept your part of the bargain, even though I know you're already doomed.' He laughed loudly but quietened immediately not to infuriate his captors beyond redemption. 'I'll keep my end of the bargain too. Another bomb is hidden in

Assam somewhere underground. It was transported long ago and was meant to only be a backup. It's much smaller but big enough to cause enough damage. That's all I know.'

They had averted a disaster only to find another one in waiting.

'Who's handling it? Who are the agents? Where do they come from?' Amjad needed all those answers immediately.

'I don't know those things. It's a different team.'

It was no time for slow conversations. Amjad needed everything as soon as possible. 'You must give us everything, Rupesh, everything you know. The pardon letter will not be of any use if I order Abhimanyu to kill you right now. You understand?'

Amjad screamed as Abhimanyu pressed his boots against Rupesh's leg wound. 'Yes, yes. I'm not one of them. I want to live. I do want to live. I have no allegiance,' Rupesh muttered through his leg pain. 'Someone named Aaliyah, she seems very important.'

'*She?*'

'Yes, a woman. I haven't seen her, but I've spoken to her a few times. She was supposed to rendezvous with the team in Guwahati and provide the final key to detonate it. Only she has it. Whoever she is, she is surely a woman.'

'How tall? Complexion? Where does she work? You must tell us everything, Rupesh, or you know it won't work out for either one of us here.'

Abhimanyu pressed his legs again.

'You must believe me.' Rupesh could barely speak through the pain this time. 'I've told you everything. They've been very protective about her identity. None of us know who she is. I was just supposed to be dropped off before Guwahati. Akhlaq and Jahangir were meant to die with the bomb.'

Amjad looked at Sonia. 'She is our detonator. If we find her, we finish this mission.'

'But we have no lead. Just his word and nothing specific.'

Amjad thought for a moment. 'Rupesh, could you recognize her voice?'

'Umm … yes. I've been taking commands from her. I know her voice.'

'Get every female agents' voice we have. Past terrorists, defectors, foreign intelligence agents, current and former—basically any foe who has ever been in the Northeast,' he said to Arup and turned to Rupesh again. 'How do we find the Bomb, Rupesh?'

The pain had run its course. Rupesh had gotten used to it. His voice was calmer. 'Look for abandoned underground bunkers. That's what they used. Look for even minor radiation surges. Whatever technology they have, I'm told the radiation surges whenever it's set up in a new place or removed from the bunker. They've managed to subdue it but not eliminate it. In normal course, it may not be alarming spikes, but a spike will still occur.'

The Northeast didn't contain too many underground bunkers, so it should be easy for ISRO to track radiation surges. 'If we focus on a few locations, we can even trace back in time through our records.' Amjad eyed the ISRO Chief.

'ISRO tracks all surges. Natural or unnatural, nothing escapes our eyes in the sky even when the cause is unknown. Though the exact source can only be ascertained once we visit the site.'

They had a starting point. 'Arup, can you get Rupesh to us? We have another mission for the MARCOS.' Amjad shifted gears into the operational maneuvers.

Army backups swooped in the area around the Teesta River bridge, and a transport chopper lifted the bomb while the terrorists were taken in another MI-35 to the Guwahati command center. Abhimanyu, Akram, and Siddhartha along with other commandos got into their helicopter, wondering where to begin next. Meanwhile, General Arup had been awfully silent for some time. Amjad curiously searched for him and finally found him behind an almirah at one end of the room, looking for something.

Arup opened a folder titled Project Diamond containing multiple designs of a bomb that could be just as small as Rupesh had explained and could prevent radiations even when activated. 'I know what Rupesh is talking about. Ghost bombs.'

Everyone stopped doing whatever they were doing as Arup projected his laptop onto the overhead screen. 'Chinese military had been testing it as part of their Project Diamond. These are contained in a stabilized graphene uranium-isotope shield. The uranium isotope in the shield acts like a continuous absorber of the radiations while carbon collogues keep it stable.'

'They haven't stopped the radiation; they've just created a shield that absorbs it before it's emitted,' Amjad gathered.

Arup nodded. 'Which means, unlike the first truck, we can't detect it even when it's activated.'

'However, the shield itself emits radiations whenever it requires setting up in any new place or requires to be moved,' Sonia reasoned.

'While we can't detect the bomb through typical radiations scanners in the sky, we can review the logs and overlay all the minor leaks ISRO has detected and overlay these with all the old or known defunct bunker locations.'

'Something of this size can't be hidden easily. We need to flush them out one by one,' Sonia concluded.

'She's right. I can get my ground sweepers on it. We have three of them in Eastern command.' Ground sweepers were low altitude helicopters with built-in technology to scan underground objects.

It was a good idea, but Amjad was nervous, wondering if they had sufficient time to swoop through the entire

East even with the targeted search. 'We need more than that. We can't go around sweeping the East.'

After a few moments, Arup broke the silence. 'Maybe we need to think like them. What would you do if your plan A of detonating a ten-ton nuke doesn't succeed? What would be your plan B?'

'Their idea is to do as much damage as possible to a city. So, I would place it near a city so I can transfer it quickly to the city and my detonator, who is in the same area, can still detonate the bomb,' Amjad added.

'In this case, we know the detonator is somewhere in or near Guwahati, so the second bomb should also be near Guwahati,' Abhimanyu added.

'Worst case, it would be farther from the city to hide it from the security forces. They'd still need to bring it into the city because the detonator is there,' Amjad said.

'That leaves us with the outskirts of Guwahati. That's where we start our search then spread to all other city outskirts once Guwahati is secure,' Arup finished, and Amjad nodded. 'Abhimanyu, report to the Guwahati command center. Stay on standby till we find the next specific lead.'

'Roger that.' Abhimanyu switched on his rotors and lifted off for the command center.

By the time Abhimanyu and his team reached the Guwahati control room, Amjad and Arup's men had put together a few pieces of the puzzle. The joint taskforce had generated workable leads. 'So, what have we got?'.

'We found the second truck,' Sonia said with delight. 'The ghost bomb came in from Bangladesh.'

'On the road again?'

'Yes. We took cues from the truck we just captured and designed an approximate version of what a truck carrying this ghost bomb on those roads would look like. Smaller but heavier due to the weight of the shield, it couldn't go unnoticed.'

'Border Intelligence had reported seeing a similar truck around a month back at the Bangladesh border. The owner of the registered number is a rubber plantation worker in Meghalaya,' Arup added.

'The plantation is owned by Rakesh Agrawal, a well-known cross-border smuggler. Arrested thrice by local police, each time, his connections bailed him out,' Amjad added then asked playfully, 'Guess who called him five times in the last two years?'

It had to be someone important; Abhimanyu waited for the answer.

'Azghar.' It all added up now. 'Rakesh received five calls from Afghanistan from the same area where RAW suggests Azghar operates. I don't think it's a coincidence. Rakesh has the resources to get something this big smuggled across the border, and Azghar must have found out.'

After a moment of silence, he added, 'I suspect Rakesh didn't have any leverage to say no to someone like Azghar even if he knew what was inside the consignment.'

Images appeared on the screen. 'We found two images of this truck in our surveillance records,' the ISRO Chief added. 'First one was shot just before it entered the Indian borders at the Agartala checkpoint, and the second photo was clicked in the forests of Meghalaya, after which the truck was never seen again.' He handed the photographs to Amjad, Arup, and Abhimanyu.

Amjad's phone buzzed, and he excused himself. Two minutes later, he returned with a lot more confidence on his face. 'My guys have picked up Rakesh Agrawal. It didn't take him long to breakdown with a gun to his mouth. He has confessed he took a handsome payment to transport the explosives, still under the impression it was just a regular weapon cache. Rakesh has no idea he just smuggled a nuclear bomb into his country. ISRO has also confirmed it's the same truck our surveillance spotted.'

Whoever was orchestrating the mission had put in a herculean effort to bring together so many moving parts. The network was getting wider at every turn, which only made Abhimanyu's task tougher. This was not just a terrorist attack but a call for war.

'We just intercepted a nuke that entered India via Nepal, and now we know the Bangladeshi border has been compromised as well. This cannot just be a terrorist outfit. It must be something bigger than that—someone with wider connections, deeper pockets, access to high technology, and an ability to command respect across allegiances.' Akram's doomsday scenario showed his frustration, which was the last thing Abhimanyu needed right now.

'War against whom? By whom?' Abhimanyu regarded him with raised eyebrows for doing what politicians do—speculate. However, as much as he hoped Akram was wrong, the planning and this scale of resource deployment had never been seen before. No country or terrorist organization alone could pull off such an act. But who was the real enemy?

Amjad saw little merit in the argument. He was pragmatic enough not to be swayed by such theories and focus on the task ahead instead. 'I wouldn't worry about it. As far as the data goes, we're dealing with another open nuke and a terrorist organization who's better prepared than last time.'

The ball was in ISRO's court. All eyes were on Uday now. Uday had been the ISRO Chief for over a year and was the only civilian face in the room. He stayed in touch with Arnab Roy, Head of the Tunnel and also Shankar, the national security advisor, for occasional support, but this was altogether a new experience for him. He had never been in a command room on a live situation. The pressure of any misstep leading to a catastrophe was unnerving. Thankfully, Uday had managed to hold his own so far. 'We've detected a location in Meghalaya with minor spikes in radiation. It was too weak to be caught by radar, but a manual check picked it up. There is nothing natural nearby to suggest it was organic, so we need a reconnaissance team to check the site.'

Amjad eyed Abhimanyu and nodded.

He collected his gear. 'The area has large swathes. We'll need your on-ground troops for combing operations. As many as we can get.'

Given the scale of the leaks so far, it was a foregone conclusion that the detonator knew about the capture of their first nuke. Rupesh said they had twenty-four hours. They would need twelve hours to diffuse the nuke safely, which left them with less than twelve hours. In that time, they had to find it and secure it.

Armed with nothing more than a vague location, MARCOS and the army commandos boarded Abhimanyu's MI-35M for another tryst with destiny. Neutralizing an enemy was an easy task, but search operations in such large swathes were a different game altogether. Paucity of time meant specialized search teams didn't have time to fly in from New Delhi and then for MARCOS to move in and neutralize the threat. The MARCOS had to do it both.

'Happy hunting,' Amjad said, and the MARCOS flew into the horizon.

Twenty minutes passed as Abhimanyu flew next to the Guwahati Shillong highway—the most probable route for any truck to move into Guwahati. They were in Meghalaya now. However, they hadn't spotted anything of significance yet.

'For once, I hope the forest cover was thinner,' Akram remarked.

'Arup, have you guys found anything yet?'

'We're trying to get a fix on all the coordinates,' Uday chipped in. 'We have multiple locations that our algorithm has pinged. The number of iterations can't be done manually in such a short time. We're now running it past Altoc, the fastest supercomputer in India. It's a game of probability now.'

The line went silent for a moment. 'Even with the night goggles, this forest cover will trouble us,' Abhimanyu acknowledged Akram's point.

The mics echoed, and Uday's voice came in sharp. 'Altoc has given us the first probable location. Coordinates are 33.20 and 66.80. This is the area where the first radiation leak was detected almost a month ago. It's around fifty kilometers from your location.'

Abhimanyu pushed forward the collective lever to reach a top speed of 335 kph and reach the location in just nine minutes. No one could see anything except the thick cover of tropical moist deciduous forests covering the highlands. Amongst the most rained areas in the world, these hills were luscious green.

'We're in the forest,' Akram quipped. 'We can't see anything but the trees. Even daylight wouldn't help us here.' He was probably right.

Abhimanyu hovered above the location and took wide-angled turns to spot anything under the tree cover but to no avail. 'We're just losing time doing this. The angles aren't helping either,' Abhimanyu said into the mics, frustrated.

Stress was taking its toll on even Amjad. 'Arup, why didn't anyone get serious about it a month ago and try to locate these locations?'

Amjad was furious at himself more than Arup.

Arup knew it had slipped through the cracks, just like many other leads. The resources needed to follow all the protocols were never there, but why would the bureaucrats in the defense ministry care? 'Given the location, it was thought to be an abnormal case of terrestrial radiation. The center for geospatial mapping came out with a few images after two weeks. They were inconclusive. We needed a ground recce, but such missions require special gear, and the approval from the ministry never came. You know how it is with the south block. No one gets serious until there is an active emergency.'

'It better be just a case of terrestrial radiations. Heads will roll in the ministry otherwise,' a frustrated Amjad said.

'We don't have time to wait for the radiation search team to do on-ground assessments,' Akram said on coms.

Amjad was still thinking. 'I'm sure the defense ministry still has not sanctioned the original request for on-ground surveillance.'

Arup nodded in affirmative, watching Amjad.

Amjad stood. 'This is a classified mission, and I use my authority as class-four lead to sanction the MARCOS to conduct a ground recce. Use your protective suits.'

Arup realized Amjad was putting himself at risk of a court martial if his judgement was proven wrong—but so were the ways of a true leader.

Abhimanyu was just waiting for the command. They were already geared in their protective suits. 'We're going in.'

Uday returned to the room, and all eyes turned to him. 'I have two more locations. Satellite images show they have lesser forest cover. One is en route to the other from your current location.'

'Send us the locations,' Abhimanyu said.

'34.60 and 66.80 is the first one. 35.80 and 66.90 is the next one. They're in the plains between the hills. If we were to believe the game of probabilities, Altoc is confident that if a second nuke indeed exists, it has to be in one of these three locations.'

Akram and Siddhartha got back into the chopper after they found nothing in the forests, and Abhimanyu rushed to the second location. He flew at top speed, and it took him just ten minutes to reach the second location. The moorland covered in heather was a sight to behold in good visibility, but there was no sign of any bunker or any sort of storage facility. Was it worth going down? It was a cruel tradeoff between time and certainty, so Abhimanyu asked Uday, 'Tell me, Chief, which of the two location has the higher probability as per our friend Altoc?'

'The last one. The one at 35.80 and 66.90. Nearest to the city, not far from the highway and no human civilization in many kilometers around it.'

Abhimanyu realized they had no time. They could never reach to the third location themselves. Swinging at an obtuse, the MI-35 came out of the circular motion and raced straight ahead. 'Arup, you'll have to get your troops to do a second check here. I don't think anything's here. We're going to the last one.'

'We have your back. Nearest team to be onsite to join you on your last check. Dispatching another team to 34.60, 66.80 for a verification.'

Abhimanyu scanned the monitor and tagged the last location.

Meanwhile, the army's combing operations in city centers hadn't yielded much yet. Soldiers on foot and in Jeeps were combing the cities to no avail. Sweeper choppers were moving in on probable locations one by one, but an operation of this scale had never ever been attempted, even in the wargames. They would need as much luck as capability to reach the finish line. MARCOS realized if Altoc was indeed right, by law of exclusion, the nuke would be in the last location. If they reached the spot in time—before the terrorists left—it was certain they would have to deal with the nuke.

Akram and Siddhartha nervously eyed each other. Akram removed the photo of his wife while Siddhartha looked skyward, seeking more courage.

'Alpha, India coming in. We're on ground zero. We're going in.'

Amjad had an eerie feeling they must be at the end of this relentless chase. If not, they wouldn't have much time left anyway. So, whether by intuition or by hope, it was the end of the rope for them. 'Be aware; hostiles expected.' The terrorists had done years of planning, and they wouldn't be neutralized without a fierce fight.

Abhimanyu started his dive in multiple rounds at an angle to locate any hostiles before they landed. He knew it was better to take them out from the air using these angles rather than on ground with his body in the firing line. He focused the backup light machinegun recalibrated to have just enough firepower to kill a human but not harm the nuke. The hostiles should have fired by now. The continuous hovering motion would have created panic if there was indeed anyone underneath. Abhimanyu concluded they were not here. He scanned the horizon.

Even at night, the hills were undoubtedly beautiful.

'Nature has perfectly curated these plains that the hills guard,' Akram said, referring to the inherent symmetry of the forestlands.

'It's difficult to believe these plains and hills are so symmetrical,' Abhimanyu remarked.

Siddhartha recalled his mountain warfare manuals. 'The rivulets decide the symmetry here. Lines of trees grow along the rivulets. You can't see the rivulets, but you can make out where they flow. The density thins out as you move from the rivulets. Along the rivulet, it's almost a parallel line.' But with the night goggles, they could see at least some of the rivulets.

'All but one place. Nine o'clock,' Abhimanyu retorted as the helicopter turned with his eyeline. Abhimanyu curiously flew over the location and noticed something wrong with the trees—perhaps a path underneath. It would be very unnatural here. But they couldn't see much else under the dark sky, so Abhimanyu took another wide angle cut from the right to have better visibility. At the lowest point, he activated the flashlights and saw a sudden movement in the trees, and one of the army commandos instinctively opened fire. 'Stop! Stop! I see antelopes! No hostiles!'

'I see something more,' Akram said.

Abhimanyu lowered the chopper, and they were shocked as he controlled the fan blades from chopping the tree branches, leaves flying off. 'A storage tank.' As the helicopter neared the tank, the antelopes ran from the storage tank into the woods. It was large enough to store a miniaturized nuke and small enough to hide it from the satellites under this thick tree cover. The storage tank was exactly where Abhimanyu would have hidden it if it were him. 'Go! Go! go!' His fingers gave the cue to unload.

Akram, Siddhartha, and two other army commandos got in line to repel the ropes. The tree covers made it hard to locate the ground exactly. If they went in with the rope without a target landing site, the rope could get stuck in the branches, risking everyone's life on the helicopter.

Akram decided to land where he could see—on top of the tree itself. He descended first. There was more noise as he landed on the trees.

Siddhartha surveyed with his night binoculars. The antelopes were now standing far away and just observing. 'It's the antelopes. They're scared. No other movement yet.'

The commandos held back to give Akram the air cover as he climbed down the tree. Akram landed on the ground, focused on the tank. He did a three-sixty-degree recce and signaled others to climb down. In less than two minutes, three commandos had descended the rope then climbed down the tree one by one.

Army commandos quickly established a perimeter around the area, and the MARCOS carefully approached the oval green storage tank. The antelopes had gone now.

Akram saw a broken antelope carcass. The flesh was rotting but not too old. 'It's not been killed by an animal.' The muscles were shredded, as if hit by a mine. Akram noticed the lack of any teeth marks or muscle tear one would expect if a wild animal had killed it. Perhaps the antelopes had triggered a mine. Akram approached the dome with ducked steps and noticed a lot of damage to the ground. Broken stones and tree parts lay all around the tank. 'It was indeed hit by a mine.' He soon found the mine crater. It also meant this was no ordinary storage tank.

'That's the reason the trees are bent here—a rope mine. The antelopes triggered it, and now we have a crater around the dome,' Siddhartha said.

'And a dead animal that died for no fault of his own.' Akram was pained, but there was no time to lose.

Akram and Siddhartha circled the storage tank a few times, and after ensuring no more mines existed, they crossed over.

'Careful,' Akram warned Siddhartha, pointing toward a snapped mine wire. 'Of course, a dead wire now.'

Siddhartha moved the radiation meter in a circular motion above the tank. It immediately showed a spike up to five hundred rems—almost as much as a normal human body would receive in ten years—high enough to suggest the presence of a nuke here but low enough the satellites wouldn't have detected it. 'The satellites must have detected the spikes only when the shield was being recalibrated.'

Even with their suits, they couldn't stay here long. Akram hovered his scanner over the tank to pick its elemental composition. This was a graphene uranium shield.

The data appeared on the screen at the Guwahati command center. 'Exactly what I was talking about,' Arup said. 'Ninety-nine percent carbon and one percent uranium isotope. That's what the Chinese have been working on.'

'But where are the terrorists?' Amjad asked.

Akram opened the tank to find it empty. However, a hot wave hit him, and the meter spiked immediately. He instinctively closed the tank. 'That's the heat blast from uranium traces. The bomb was definitely here.'

It also meant they had narrowly missed it. Abhimanyu swore to himself in frustration.

'I can see some tyre marks here. They look quite fresh,' an army commando guarding the perimeter said.

Akram rushed to the spot and dipped his fingers into it. The soil was still not settled. The commando was right. He patted the commando and announced on the coms, 'The marks are fresh. Not more than a few hours old. They shouldn't have gone far.'

'Scan the area. Look for any more marks,' Amjad said through the earbuds.

'They've cleaned the area well, sir. The mine may have destroyed any evidence left anyway. However, the tank structure looks sturdy. Should find something there if we get lucky.' Akram was acknowledging these terrorists' professionalism. Transporting a nuke without state support was no joke, and they had done well so far.

The team scanned the area with laser swipes and fed the data to the Guwahati control room where a lab team ran a live check on the fingerprint database in real time, something Abhimanyu didn't see even during the Chennai attack. But technology fell short to close the last mile on such missions, and each time, it was the men on the ground who helped them get closer to the bomb. Abhimanyu understood it well and knew they had to close in on the terrorists as soon as possible.

Akram noticed a thick wire disappearing underground. It was not a mine wire; that would be thinner. He slowly followed the wire, and it led him to a tree fifty meters from the dome. The wire went up the tree along the trunk, but nothing was on top of the tree. They slowly pulled down the wire with ease, for nothing was obstructing it at the other end—none of the usual communication equipment or transistor or even a hook. He noticed some markings and cuts on the wire's end though. Something from training struck him. 'It's a World War-era antenna used to transmit codes. It has a copper bolt. Not very clear but has a long range. They must have used it because it is impossible to detect these.'

'Why?'

'No one tracks these frequencies anymore,' Akram said into the coms.

It made sense to use them. Abhimanyu had a glimmer of hope. They had a tail now.

'Get the bolt's basic elemental composition. Sonia, map the frequencies for it,' Amjad said, and Sonia nodded in affirmation.

If they found the frequencies the terrorists used, they could interfere in their communications, even eavesdrop on them. Siddhartha rushed to the spot with his laser sweeper.

'Sonia, scan all the messages at all frequencies compatible with these antennas. I doubt if our satellites can still track them, but some of the older satellites might work.'

Siddhartha's laser sweep data helped Sonia zero in on the frequencies in less than a minute. Akram was right. It could transit very low frequencies, also known as VLF. These frequencies had lost all favor by the 1970s. Even third-world armies considered them outdated.

Amjad, for once, was lost as he tried to make sense of it. Surely, a nuclear mission had to rely on more than a mere copper antenna. 'Not if you tune it beforehand.'

Copper was one of the most common material used to transmit shortwaves at set frequencies. For many decades, international spies had used shortwave stations, but it lost to newer technologies. It was an efficient way to transmit encrypted messages on set frequencies with set protocols. They could be silent all day and still come alive with seemingly incorrigible tones or voices or even songs. They could include Morse codes, nursery rhymes, or even a musical that would hardly make any sense to sane people but carry lot of encrypted information. It could still deploy language ciphers, sequences, encryption, decryption, and other statecrafts of international espionage. Amjad realized its ingenuity lay in its simplicity. Most countries had stopped using them, owing to availability of more sophisticated and cheaper technologies. Resource constraints and algorithmic optimizations only meant lesser people were dedicated to track these lines. Gradually, most countries stopped tracking it altogether. These fedayeen were trained by old-fashioned techniques.

Amjad could feel the game levelling up further and decided to return to pure basics. 'We'll have to track all the frequencies. That will require a lot of bandwidth.' Amjad wiped some sweat off his forehead.

Sonia knew this could only be done manually. They'd need to check all the radio frequencies to the second decimal.

'Checking all the frequencies at all times would require a lot, a lot of people,' Amjad muttered, internalizing his own thoughts.

'Even if we do this, it will work only if they use these frequencies again,' Abhimanyu said.

'They haven't left too long ago, so we still have some time to track them through these signals. The detonator would still need to connect with them in Guwahati. They will use it,' Akram said while following the trail of tyre marks as far as they went.

Only one institution had that kind of a bandwidth, and Amjad glanced at Arup.

'You don't need to give me that look. I'll ask my communication specialists to track as many frequencies as they can,' he said, still unsure if it would really help.

All army units had at least one communication specialist by design. Their task was to scan the locally active frequencies, gather intelligence, and keep the base safe. One of the most mundane jobs in the army, communication specialists had to beat the monotony of radio channels over many months, sometimes even years, to catch the one signal which could make all the difference. In the best-case scenario, their jobs would lead them to preempt a terrorist attack or a local rebellion. Today was different though. In the best-case scenario, they could prevent a nuclear war. His boys would be thrilled to hunt it down.

Amjad raised his hand, acknowledging Arup's support. It wouldn't be easy to align so many army bases in such short notice, but at least they were ready to try.

CHAPTER 18

HEART STRIKE

ISI Safehouse, Pakistan

A handmade cigar had much better texture and was more effective than any branded product. Bilal Masoud picked up his cigar filled with premium Afghani weed called Garda Kush and gently lit it. It was prepared from the Afghan Kush, found only in the Hindu Kush mountains and famous for its high resin content. Owing to its rarity and powerful sedating effects, it was accessible only to the most discerning elites. It required both a well-developed taste and well-built connections to cut corners and source it. Bilal had received a pack of these cigars from one Afghani warlord after ISI had rewarded them with a million-dollar assistance. Thanks to his diplomatic skills, Bilal had brokered many such deals in the region. His exploits as a young spy in India had earned him the respect needed to transverse effectively through these networks. Everyone was more than happy to lend him an ear, even on topics the generals and warlords despised.

Bilal had done well for himself so far, but this was a moment of crisis. A meticulously planned mission had gone wrong. After he was compromised in New York, the people who had placed heavy bets on him had reprimanded him. This mission couldn't have gone wrong at any cost. The infidels had to pay. God's wrath had to be brought upon the negligent and hopeless people who worked tirelessly against the well-being of Bilal and his community. Unfortunately, the infidels had managed to stay ahead despite the head start Bilal had got them.

Bilal's lieutenants entered with some more bad news. 'They've caught the first truck and perhaps all three of our men. We can't connect to any one of them.'

Five years of planning and millions in investments had resulted in an arrest. It was not a temporary setback but a failure with several long-term implications. His sponsors weren't kind to failure. Further, any evidence linking it to them would be a diplomatic catastrophe. Bilal needed to calm himself. He huffed and puffed quick ones to rest his mind as Russel, an Uzbek recruit, and Shaheen, a Syrian ex-army commando, watched him nervously. Bilal had recruited and trained them personally, and they were his trusted aides, just like the ones before them whom Bilal had to gun down as a punishment for a failure. Bilal ruled by fear. He had a notorious reputation but working under him was still an honor. If one failed his honor, they deserved to die, but if one passed it, they would go places due to his connections.

'How did the Indians get to know about the truck? Didn't we disable the disk completely?'

'We did, Janaab. Our source confirmed it had been completely deleted.'

'Our source lied to us,' Bilal said and puffed a few more. 'Bloody Indians. Bunch of incompetent fools.' Ever since the Indians had compromised him, the sword was hanging over his head. Then they took away Khalid. Bilal had to activate a hibernating agent long before his due time just to delete the contents of the hard disk. It was a risk reserved for more opportune circumstances, for compromising the mole's cover could jeopardize the whole operation. Bilal's mistake had also kept Russel and Shaheen alive so far. Thankfully, no one could attribute the setbacks to them completely, yet.

Russell and Shaheen tried to speak, but Bilal continued, 'What will I answer to, Al Malik? First, it was the nuisance in New York, then at the border, and now they catch the truck.'

'If I may say, sir, we still have a hibernating module. By God's grace, they will be successful and bring down God's wrath on the Indians,' Russel said with a trembling voice.

Bilal knew he was scared but right. Al Malik never took chances with his investments, so the backup had been in place long before needed. All they had to do was to wait, because the backup was foolproof. 'We needn't worry. Indians have no inkling who's coming their way. Aaleyah will bring us glory.'

'Aaleyah is in the field on this, Janaab?' Shaheen asked, pleasantly surprised.

Bilal nodded.

Shaheen's confidence was back and so was his smile. Aaleyah was a title given to only the best of the agents. It was earned through great sacrifice and skill. 'That's right. It's Aaleyah's game now. We need to provide every help we can to Aaleyah. Else, this will be our end.' Shaheen's smile shrunk.

'This will be my end,' Bilal said slowly. The stakes were very high for him as well. If they failed, the axe could fall on him. The clocks chimed, and the orbs circled over him. Bilal finished his cigar just in time, as his master awaited him. He carefully gathered his thoughts. Still under the influence of the cigar, he was convinced he had a safe way out. He stood from his chair and walked to the basement.

Shaheen and Russel stayed back.

Al Malik operated behind the veil of anonymity, for he was truly serving only the God himself. Public adulation was not what he yearned, so very few knew his true identity.

Bilal had met Al Malik twenty-five years ago. Back then, Abdullah Bahri had been an oil billionaire's reclusive young son who moved effortlessly amongst the billionaires of America, royals of the Middle East, and heads of the governments for his business enterprise. No one figured Bahri's inclinations to connect with the underworld and his tendency to give dole outs to who he called, "the real downtrodden." To this end, he looted the governments and corporations alike. As per him, nation governments were corrupt on their own—ethically, morally, and religiously by design. These nation's governments had become a machine for making the rich richer. The downtrodden were used as raw material keep, feeding their production lines. This narrative helped him build a network of underworld entities across the globe. They funded anyone who supported them, be it dictators, military leaders, or ragtag democratic governments. Bahri funded them and derived extreme pleasure from their corruptibility. They were a shame on humanity and had to be eliminated one by one. They didn't stand true to their own religious identities and rituals and succumbed to the temptations of sex, alcohol, and money. They were all infidels.

On the other hand, Bilal Masoud had been a rising spy twenty-five years ago. He accidentally landed on information that led him to Abdullah's linkages to fedayeen networks in the Middle East. After understanding the true intentions of his work, Bilal knew Abdullah was a friend to have for the long term. But he was very hard to spot or contact, for he ensured all his meetings were out of public eye. It took Bilal five years to plot his chance meeting with Abdullah at a billionaire's afterparty in Las Vegas. Bilal made his move and introduced himself to Abdullah. To gain Abdullah's trust, he shared the information he had landed upon five years ago. Abdullah took kindly that Bilal had sat on the information for five years just to meet him. To test Bilal, Abdullah gave him a tougher task.

Abdullah had been in the US for round tripping the illegal funds to the Middle East and asked Bilal to spy on a banks' managing director. If caught, Bilal could lose his diplomatic immunity and spend decades in the infamous US prisons. However, he accepted the task and unearthed the deeper ecstasies of the managing director. With several photographs in compromising positions, Abdullah managed to negotiate a deal for the US bank to issue credit to entities in the Middle East via their Dubai branch in exchange for assets placed in collateral at the US branch. Only later did Bilal discover these entities were front charities for many of the armed groups operating in the wider Middle East. Abdullah had successfully delegated the headache of round tripping the American regulators to an American bank.

That was the first and the last time Bilal had met Abdullah in person. Abdullah had made it clear that he shouldn't even try to meet him again, that it would not be taken lightly. That was the way Abdullah operated. Once he trusted someone, he preferred them to operate as independently as possible. Abdullah provided resources and push from the topmost levels wherever required to get the job done through his contacts. His extensive network also acted as a check on all the independent assets, and over decades, he had perfected the model. Rigorous cross references and unforgiving ruthlessness had insured no one dared cross him. The ones he liked were bestowed with rewards. Bilal was amongst them. Thanks to Abdullah, he had an envious career in the

Pakistani Army. Every time Bilal completed a major mission for Abdullah, he was promoted internally. Bilal's network and the reward system worked flawlessly. Abdullah had his higher ups in confidence, even then Bilal could never pinpoint their identities. Abdullah's statecraft was perfect, and Bilal knew he was just one cog in the wheel. Today, Abdullah had initiated the videocall; he rarely did it. Audio messages and couriers were enough. It was an important conversation, and Bilal hoped Al Malik gave him more time to show what he can truly accomplish.

As usual, Al Malik was in time and on topic. 'I hear the first nuke has been captured. Is that true?' A black figure appeared on the hazy screen. Abdullah didn't want to be seen.

'Yes, Al Malik.' There was an awkward silence. 'Give me another chance, please.'

'You had your chance. We spent millions of dollars on it. Hard earned money of people dedicated to our cause and you have failed them.'

Bilal needed a chance at the mission, a chance at life. He kneeled and looked up at the hazy black figure in dim light. 'I have positioned Aaleyah close to the mission's location. I'll activate Aaleyah, and the glory will be ours. Give me just one more chance, Al Malik.'

Abdullah Bahir went silent for a moment. He trusted Aaleyah. The mission couldn't go wrong if Bilal had managed to get her in the right location. 'They can't defeat Aaleyah. Not this one.'

Bilal gained confidence to stand and felt a little relieved. 'The mission will be over before they know what has hit them.'

Al Malik was confident, but something bothered him. The silhouette on the screen held its head down for a long time then raised it suddenly. 'I trust Aaleyah, but give me the facts. How do I trust that you won't handle Aaleyah the way you handled Jahangir and Akhlaq?'

Bilal had come prepared. He connected his laptop and flashed a few photographs. 'This is the safehouse they are using. We have done a recce, and tonight, we'll take it out.'

Abdullah thought for a moment. Bilal's plan was not foolproof but aimed at the right spot.

'It will demoralize them, distract them.' Bilal shoveled through the photos and put Sasha's photo on the screen. 'She will be our ticket.'

'Do we have enough men nearby?'

'We do, Your Highness. Just give us one more chance.'

Abdullah Bahir wasn't a man to take chances, but this time, the odds felt tempting. He eyed Sasha's photo again. 'If you fail this time ...'

'I understand. Your Highness'—Bilal bowed—'king of kings, my life is in your hands.'

'You have one more day.'

'Ji Janaab.'

They had to attack Bagyidaw's without wasting any time. That would give them a distraction for long enough to execute the second attack.

'One more thing. I want Aaleyah alive at any cost. You have her code.'

Al Malik, alias Abdullah Bahir, left Bilal perplexed. Aaleyah was only a title given by the fraternity to the best-trained spies. In his younger days, Bilal had himself tried for that title and failed, thrice. They received the best training across the globe and executed the most impactful attacks. The New York twin tower attack, London blasts, Madrid train blasts, or even the Mumbai local blasts each had an Aaleyah working on it tirelessly in the background. However, they were never caught. They were the faceless warriors who could appear and disappear just as swiftly from the sights. No one knew their identities except the Al Maliks. The process was foolproof.

It was still out of the ordinary for Al Malik to indulge in protecting someone on a mission—especially an Aaleyah, for they were bred for the ultimate sacrifice if needed. Bilal checked the code Abdullah Bahir had given him. It had the mark of the Circle, the mark that made him fret. Only Aaleyah knew that code. Whoever Aaleyah was, Al Malik had a vested interest in keeping Aaleyah alive. It was a blessing in disguise for him. If he executed plan B well, Al Malik would still restore his honor and rewards. So he decided to arrange another module as a backup to the backup with only one task. It had to extract Aaleyah at all costs.

Guwahati Airport

Arup had sent a red memo to all the army units. The next lead was not too far. The Indian Army had last used a red memo in the Kargil war. War was imminent, and all army unit heads had realized it, despite being unaware of the specific threat. Communication specialists had been put to work to man as many frequencies as possible. The MARCOS returned from their recce mission. Midnight was still thirty minutes too far in what was proving to be the longest night of Abhimanyu's career. In the safety of the base, Abhimanyu relaxed his guard and gathered his thoughts. He shook hands with Lieutenant Abhishek and Lieutenant Shikhar, the army commandos who had proven their mettle alongside MARCOS and patted their back.

'This way.'

Military Communications Officer Major Bikram Singh handed Abhimanyu a dossier with all the updates they had gathered till then. He looked confident. 'We've detected twenty-four channels so far. Most of them are local radio channels, but five of them are privately managed, hence, are active only intermittently.'

Abhimanyu took the file. Local channels, sports channels, tribal folk music channels, and lines maintained by NGOs dominated the list. Eleven channels had operators whose identities were not known to the agencies. It was a lot to not know. The local army intelligence should have highlighted it earlier, but then Abhimanyu reflected, no one even tracked these channels anymore.

Bikram took Abhimanyu and his team to the control room where Arup and the others were busy interpreting all the data coming in from the various army bases.

With a gentle smile, Amjad acknowledged their work on the first nuke but quickly refocused on the big screen. The mission was not over yet. 'Satellites haven't detected anything in the ultra-high frequency bands.' It wasn't unexpected. All satellites had migrated out of these frequencies to the more commonly used ones long ago. 'Army units have traced some rogue signals from Assam, but they were not active for long enough to trace the origin.'

'If not the frequencies, can we get some satellite images?' Abhimanyu asked.

'Even in the best case, the images will only have dense forests.'

Abhimanyu was confused, so Bikram clarified. 'A tag is something distinct which satellites can lock onto in the night cover. Then the algorithms take over. It could be as simple as a torch light or a vehicle.'

Abhimanyu scanned the private channels on the list. 'Tell me more about these five privately managed channels and their locations.'

'Different parts of Northeast, all with dense forest cover. Many ham radio operators exist in this part of the world.'

'Do we have the coordinates?'

'Difficult to pinpoint the exact location, but many of these originate in the West Siang mountains.' Amjad watched Abhimanyu's reaction.

'Weren't you holidaying there?' Siddhartha said.

'Yeah, on my leave,' Abhimanyu replied, the irony not lost on Amjad. Abhimanyu took the file from Bikram. All the frequencies used were in the VLF band. 'All five came from forests?'

'One of them is from Guwahati area. The rest, yes.'

Abhimanyu saw where the team was going with this.

'The signal from Guwahati has moved its location consistently. The towers typically have a radius of fifteen to twenty miles. In a city with a million plus people, it'll take us many hours of satellite surveillance coupled with on-ground intelligence to pinpoint the exact location in the city. In the end, it could just be a ham operator moving around the city.'

'So, we target the four others.'

'Yes, that's what we've planned. One of them is from the Nagaland mountains and the other three from West Siang mountains.'

Abhimanyu had only one question now, and it was for the ISRO Chief.

Uday knew exactly what he had on his mind. 'We've been surveilling all of them. The Nagaland signal has led us to some pictures, but they're too hazy.' He placed the pictures on the table containing at least five people sitting around a bonfire; nothing else was visible. 'We're waiting to get better angles with our satellites to get a picture with higher clarity.'

'How much more time will you need?' Abhimanyu asked.

'Not much. Fifteen minutes.'

They could wait for fifteen minutes. He nodded, and everyone resumed work. The thought of the other three signals from West Siang mountains was on top of everyone's mind, but they had nothing on it yet.

Amjad was wary of losing precious time.

Arup couldn't bear the uncertainty and returned to follow up with the communication teams of several army units but got no new information from them.

Everyone was tensed to the hilt, and they waited with bated breath for fifteen minutes, which passed as hours. All eyes watched the big screen. The satellite rendered the image, pixel by pixel. Halfway through the photo, it was clear these were armed militants. Most of them had machineguns hanging on their shoulders.

'These could be our guys.' They even had a truck parked next to them. 'What's in the truck?' Abhimanyu asked.

'We can't know that unless they open it,' Uday responded.

Amjad noticed a pixel on the truck. 'Can you zoom in on the right side of the truck?' One frame deeper and he said, 'These are not our guys.' As the photo zoomed in, the flag was clearer to the others. They were the men of the Naga United Army. 'These are just a bunch of militants.'

'But we need to know what's in the truck. What if the local work was handed over to them? They are no friend of ours either,' Arup said.

As they wondered what the next step could be, one of the militants looked skyward, as if he was watching them. The other one stood and pointed toward the stars.

Even Amjad looked nervously at Abhimanyu and Arup.

'I would so want to have the audio on that,' Siddhartha said.

The ISRO Chief shrugged. It was not possible without an on-ground team.

After the militants completed their conversation, two of them approached the truck and opened the slider. All eyes stared at the screen. One of them went inside, and the other one removed a long knife. The first militant pulled a goat from the truck and dragged it to a nearby rock, where the second one slit its throat.

'Dinnertime!' Arup said in frustration.

'He was checking the moon's alignment with the stars. We have just got into the Naga New Year,' Amjad added.

'Back to square one,' Amjad said as much in frustration as in relief for Nagaland, which was farther from Guwahati. He knew he would need his men to be on the ground to finish this, and Nagaland was not the nearest battlefield to choose.

Abhimanyu got back into his grove. 'Can you just highlight the probable areas of the other four signals?'

Sonia did; each one partially overlapped the other two.

'Now, place the timestamps where they were detected.'

Almost immediately, Abhimanyu's thought process became clear to everyone. The circle moved gradually toward Guwahati as the time passed. Why didn't it strike him earlier? 'The signal is from someone who's moving toward Guwahati.'

'And they correspond with someone every thirty minutes.' It was brilliant. Arup was damn impressed.

'Put on the timestamps of the Guwahati station also.'

Sonia did, and it was clear the two signals were talking, for they appeared together within a space of minutes. 'They are synchronized.'

'At pre-decided times,' Amjad added. They had half a smile now.

'They will talk again. Arup, get us every hand you can find in that area, and get as many communication tracking beacons live as possible. We need to track the entire Shillong-Guwahati highway.'

'Absolutely.' The enthusiasm in Arup's voice was infectious.

Everyone realized they had something tangible now. The MARCOS stood. They needed to be airborne again and be ready for the intervention when they finally found the truck.

'Load the fuel.'

Abhimanyu, Akram, Siddhartha, along with the army commandos left the control room and reloaded in the ammunition area.

Amjad walked along to ensure they were briefed properly for this big mission on the longest night of their life. 'I hope this is the last mission tonight.' Amjad was more fearful than hopeful.

'Me too,' Abhimanyu said.

'We have never come across such an elaborate threat. We should be ready for surprises, some hard calls.'

Abhimanyu nodded.

'From what we've seen so far, they won't fold without a thunder.'

Abhimanyu saw Amjad's concerns. He gave him a confident smile to assure him they were in their elements. 'I want all of you to know, what you've done so far has been exemplary, but don't let that blindside you.'

'No, no of course,' Akram responded.

'They have planned a backup on a nuclear mission. It also means they'd be willing to sacrifice far more capital—human or political,' Amjad's said, trying hard to caution them to be prepared for the worst-case scenario, to not let complacency creep in.

'Midway explosion?'

'Yes, that, and perhaps something else too. I don't know, but desperate times call for desperate measures, and when they know we have spotted their second truck as well, they'll be desperate.' Amjad realized, by simple game theory, that if the terrorists didn't have it their way, they'd try to ensure that the Indians do not have it their way either. So this time, the Indians did not just need to shock them but incapacitate them, paralyze them before they could make a move on the nuke. For this, Amjad had a plan. 'I've loaded the chopper with a box of alpha-grade tranquilizers. Keep on the masks, and don't hesitate to use them.'

Abhimanyu was not perturbed but surprised. The alpha-grade tranquilizers were made of banned chemical compounds. Its usage was confined only to the contained laboratories. Any detection by international observatory agencies would put India in a tough spot. It would be a diplomatic nightmare. They could even alter the local climatic conditions and posed long-term ecological risks. As per the standard operating procedures, a trained team would later clear the site of any traces. However, it was just theory because the tranquilizers had never been used on live missions yet. Abhimanyu knew Amjad was resourceful enough to get access to it but didn't realize he would be so eager to use it. Obviously, Amjad didn't share it with anyone in the command center, and Abhimanyu wanted to keep it that way. Only one more thought bothered Abhimanyu. 'The signals are very close to the West Siang mountains.'

'I know what's on your mind. Very close to Bagyidaw's bungalows, you mean?' Amjad could preempt his thoughts.

He nodded.

'You don't need to worry about her. I've already alerted the commandos there. Additional team of MARCOS have also been sent to Bagyidaw's. She is as much my daughter as she is your wife.'

It meant a lot to him. Amjad's hands on his shoulder acted like a balm to his stress. Amjad always had his back.

'We'll also discuss your other thought. Resolve it once you're back.'

Abhimanyu wasn't sure if he really wanted to leave everything behind. He smiled at Amjad and knew this was his last mission before retirement. 'I can't be grateful enough. Can we also just get her out of there? I know it's a tough thing to ask amongst all this, but …'

Amjad was disturbed to realize Abhimanyu was preparing for the worst-case scenario, but perhaps it was the more practical thing to do. If the nuke detonated, he didn't want Sasha anywhere near, and rightly so. 'No, no. It's not at all difficult. You're right. Instead of additional security, we'll arrange for her extraction right away. We have a large fleet of choppers. Let's use them.' On his part, Amjad could only ensure he had Sasha off his mind completely. Amjad needed his entire focus to be on just one thing—Cortex. 'Anything else on your mind?'

'I've seen assassins in those jungles, Amjad. Just to reiterate, make sure you help them well in time.' It was more an emotional appeal than a simple request from Abhimanyu.

Amjad put his hands on his shoulder and nodded. 'Leave her to me.'

Abhimanyu nodded, smiled from reassurance and finally boarded the helicopter.

'Remember …'

Abhimanyu looked back at Amjad by the chopper's hatch door.

'We are few, but what makes us different is we are also fearless. Don't let anything take that away from you.'

Those words were always motivating. He had a confident smile on his resolute face. Abhimanyu had to conquer his fears if he were to save his country. He put on his helmet, and the team thundered straight into the air to take on the orbs circling around them once again.

Few minutes into the ride, before switching off the external communications, Abhimanyu called Sasha. She might have fallen asleep by now, but it was still a good time to check on her before he got on with the long night ahead. The phone rang once, twice, and then thrice to no avail. He tried again. Nobody answered. Abhimanyu tried again. He then tried the common line. The phone rang again, but nobody responded. Even though it was late, this was unusual. With so many guards and Thapa, someone should have surely answered the common line. Even the protocols required the common lines to be kept open twenty-four hours a day. It was perhaps just a matter of coincidence but definitely ill-timed. 'Amjad, can you check on Bagyidaw's mainline? It's nonresponsive.'

Amjad was surprised. 'Sure.'

He dialed the common line and then Thapa's direct room line. The phone rang incessantly. Amjad tried to connect with the MARCOS on site, but they didn't respond either. With some anxiety, he called the backup team, who should have reached the site by now. They were unresponsive as well. It was a bad sign. At this stage however, it was even more important to keep Abhimanyu calm. Amjad couldn't pass this information to him. Abhimanyu needed to be focused on his mission, mentally and not just turn up physically. Whatever be the reason for this uncanny silence at the Bagyidaw's, the situation was a nightmare for Amjad. Five, ten, and then fifteen minutes had passed. Amjad was now desperate for an idea to get through.

Meanwhile, Abhimanyu was getting restless. 'Amjad, do you have anything?'

Amjad was out of his wits on how to handle the situation. Eventually, he decided to lie for once. 'Okay. I just confirmed with the MARCOS onsite. They're practicing a communication blackout. Standard procedure for emergencies. They should have informed us, but they decided it at the last moment. Nothing to worry about.'

CHAPTER 19
THE FLOP

Guwahati Command Center

The moonlight at midnight was not enough to spot the van that snuck up gently on the mansion in sector 50 in Noida. Inside the van, two men studied the monitors. Ravi, a software engineer from Infosys, an Indian IT behemoth, and Raja, a cyber security expert at Intel, had been asked to report at a very short notice. The corporate job was a coverup for their real job with the Indian Intelligence Bureau. Hence, they were surprised they had been asked to snoop on IB's Deputy Director Mr. Radha Narayanan's house at this hour. The men waited for the final order to infiltrate his house networks.

'Are we all set?' Amjad whispered in Sonia's ears, and she nodded. Amjad checked the time. They had fifteen minutes.

Sonia donned her hood and exited the control room. She crossed the army compound and stepped into another van outside the base. The success of this mission was critical for the success of their mission in the hills, for neutralising the enemy inside was important to regain the edge.

'What is he doing?'

'Nothing. No movement yet.' Sonia had infiltrated IB's most secure protocols to extract a comprehensive list of people in the IB who had access to the hard disk. There were three of them. She tracked all of them independently and finally traced at least four unreported signals from Deputy Director Radha's house. The frequencies didn't correspond to any of the Indian stations or intelligence services, and every time Radha got the signal, he left his home, even though it were odd hours.

Last time Radha got the signal, Sonia was determined to know its content. A digital signal specialist was stationed outside his house to catch the signal. The code simply translated to a location. Presumably, each time Radha got the messages, he left for these locations. Interestingly, the signals only arrived midnight. Today it would be a fake signal, sent by Sonia.

Amjad entered the van discreetly enough to cover his tracks. He was determined to avoid any hiccups in catching this mole. He had started planning this classified operation the moment they had realized the hard disk had been compromised in Indian custody. Deputy Director Radha was indeed a very senior person and had direct access to the hard disk. In fact, he had personally signed it out before passing it on to Sunaina after the operational team in IB had cleared it. Of course, he had enough time to delete the contents, even though, for some reason, he couldn't delete everything.

Amjad could have never gotten a warrant against the Deputy Director of Intelligence Bureau without uncivil drama—something he couldn't afford at this juncture. Head of IB Prem and even head of Border Intelligence Sunaina, who had lost an irreplaceable asset in Major General Akash, would have fumed fury at him. It was beyond his remit. Hence, Amjad decided to go solo with the people he trusted. Ravi and Raja were from Sonia's batch. They had a spotless civilian background from birth till today and good recruits for the Indian agencies. They didn't have the nerves to cross the border, but they had the corporate identity to move around multinationals unrecognized. Amjad had borrowed this modus operandi from the Chinese playbook. Today, they were on a pro bono mission.

The clock struck midnight, and Ravi pressed the key, releasing a signal at a preset frequency. Ravi and Raja had spent hours insuring their signal was accurate and passed Radha's stress test. He most likely had some sort of a code or a device to check the authenticity of the incoming signals. It had the latitudes, longitudes of a location around ten kilometers from his house in Noida sector 50. The fake signal was built from the pieces of the four original ones they had intercepted in the past few days. They fixated on the screens. Two drones at a thousand feet high waited for Raja to make his move. It was important that Radha trusted the signal. Five minutes had passed, Radha had still not left his house.

'He's normally out within five minutes once he receives the signals,' Sonia said.

Ten minutes had passed. He was still inside.

Ravi detected another signal. 'There's some sort of transmission. He's sending a message.'

'Can you read it?' Amjad was getting nervous. Perhaps Radha had detected the intrusion.

Ravi was working to get into the transmission. 'I can't. It's a completely different language. Last time, it took us more than a day to decode.'

'He has received something now,' Sonia interrupted when she saw another spike on the screen.

'His handlers. They're responding to his message,' Amjad deduced.

'There he is. Coming out from the back gate.' Sonia couldn't miss him even in the dark alleys that led from his home.

'Normally, he comes out the front gate and keeps it very simple,' Ravi said.

Amjad and Sonia did not like it. He was already behaving suspiciously, and they had to improvise, hereon.

Amjad had stationed two commandos outside Radha's house to tail him and catch him red-handed. The plan had to be changed now. 'Tango Romeo, Come in.'

'Tango Romeo, ready. Over.'

'Delivery address has changed. Watch the customer. Over.'

'Customer in sight. Over.'

It was moving too fast for Amjad's liking. 'Customer has defaulted and on the run. He may be aggressive. Maintain distance. Over.'

Radha got into his bulletproof BMW, paid for by the government, and sped from the back gate. Mindful of his surroundings, he kept an eye on the rearview mirror and side paths. Few inebriated people lined the footpaths, but no sane soul was on the road—a norm in this part of the capital at this hour. This sector was still developing, and there were many woody areas where one could hide.

The MARCOS emerged from one such tree cover. They switched off their headlights and tailed Radha while maintaining a distance of more than a kilometer. He wasn't in their sight, but the satellites had tagged his car. Ravi and Raja refused to miss him. Radha was going in exactly the opposite direction to the one Amjad had planned. It was also toward the city now. It would be hard to control an operation in the city crowd. Perhaps Radha was already playing this game now, but Amjad couldn't play along much longer. He still had nothing concrete to nail him.

Radha parked in a deserted parking area of a prominent city mall. It was not a safe place for Radha.

Being a professional, Radha could have gone to a more secure place, like his office or his handler's place, but he chose an open area in the city outskirts—a crime hotspot at midnight.

It was a bad place for Amjad as well. They couldn't interrogate him in a public place. 'Tango Charlie, bring the customer to warehouse. Avoid a scene. Over.'

The MARCOS were trailing him by a good distance and quickly moved into the fifth gear. It would still take them almost a minute to reach the mall parking.

Radha entered through the gates and was soon out of the satellite's vision. He aimlessly wandered inside the mall, ignoring the escalators, for he had been asked to take the stairs. As he climbed the stairs, he saw a group of unkempt men, most probably migrant labors, pass him.

One of them, visibly intoxicated, brushed against him in anger at Radha for disrupting his path.

Radha apologized and moved on. A moment later, a phone rang. Radha could hear it loud but didn't see it till he realized it was in his own jacket. He looked back, but the unkept men were gone. He answered the call. 'Okay … Okay, I'll be there.' Radha's hands could barely hold the phone now, for the sweat was discomforting. He took some nervous steps to the fourth floor into the food court hosting a decent crowd. Radha felt a little assured and took refuge next to the dim fire exit alley, giving him a good place to hide.

The MARCOS entered the mall. One stayed back at the exit while the other scanned the ground floor.

'Ground floor clear. No sign.'

Amjad knew Radha had something to hide or he wouldn't have given away his cover by reacting so suspiciously. Amjad had his target cornered. He wondered if they should abort the mission and wait for Radha to make a bigger mistake later. It was farfetched to expect Radha to meet his handler when he knew he had a tail. An abrupt sound interrupted his thought.

'Shots fired! Shots fired!' the MARCOS shouted into the coms.

The commotion came from the top floor of people rushing to the nearest exit possible. The silence on the stairs was broken by people cutting in on each other to get ahead. Soon, the escalators were choked. Given the hara-kiri, the emergency system had kicked in, stopping the escalators. The ran down the up-stair escalators. The MARCOS rushed to the site through the escalators against the crowd, but they were too late. Radha's body lay in a pool of blood few meters from the fire exit. The door was half open. The bullet wound hadn't pierced his body, and the only visible wound was between the shoulder blade and the spiral column. The bullet was stuck in his heart. A professional killer had shot Radha from behind at close range. The MARCOS ran to the exit, but no one was in the stairs. Then they heard the loud sound of the exit door on the ground floor. The killer had slipped out of the building.

'Suspect has escaped from the ground floor fire exit in the southwest wing.'

Sonia had the exit on her screens in Guwahati. It was impossible to spot the suspect because the mall exit lay right next to it. The killer had already mingled with the crowd, and face recognition didn't work at these resolutions at nighttime. They had lost him. Radha was the mole indeed, but they had missed the handler.

Amjad banged his fist on the caravan's table.

The MARCOS returned to the body. They unlocked Radha's phone with a simple fingerprint replica they had been carrying.

In no time, Sonia had the phone logs on her screen. Radha had sent the three-word phrase *Python is Descaled* to an unknown number. In response, he had just gotten the mall's address. Sonia tracked the unknown number to a Pakistani connection registered in Islamabad. 'That won't be enough to implicate him. No calls. No hard documents.' Sonia realized they had a bigger crisis on their hands now. The IB Deputy Director was killed without any material evidence admissible in courts. They were screwed.

Amjad gathered his thoughts. There had to be a way out. It was still a victory. Sonia had verified all of Radha's communications, and he was acting alone. They had taken down the mole, and the intelligence systems were no longer compromised. It was a much needed relieve amidst this relentless chase. Amjad thought it wouldn't be a bad idea to share the news with the forces and boost their morale. Even Abhimanyu could finally let his mind rest.

'That's weird,' Sonia said, still detecting messages transmitting to Radha's home. 'If Radha is dead and they are still contacting him on these frequencies, they still don't know he is dead.'

'Or more than one module is contacting him.' Amjad realized there was information asymmetry here, and either way, he could use it to his advantage—both internally to land the news and externally to send the terrorists in a spiral. He dialed in the Delhi Police Commissioner.

'Remember, I owed you one.'

'Yes, a medal.'

'Yes, your medal. You can have it now.'

'Never thought there was a barter possible, but if you say so.'

'It is not possible. But it can be faked. We have a situation on our hands, and you need to create an encounter scene at a mall. The medal is just an afterthought.'

'Enlighten me.'

'We caught Deputy Director of Intelligence Bureau Radha Narayanan red-handed, communicating with terrorist organizations, perhaps ISI. We shot him in the chase that ensued. We can't take the fall for it. Delhi

Police being on the outside can. Search his house and you'll find evidence. Once everyone accepts he was a mole, your medal will follow.'

'I'm not dumb Amjad. What if we don't find any evidence? What if he's innocent? You want me to take a fall for you?'

'That's not the case. They killed Radha because they knew he had been compromised. But they still don't know how he had been compromised. That's the reason his device at his home is still active and receiving signals. We need your help to delay this realization for as long as possible. Can you do that?'

Delhi Police Commissioner took his time to trust it, but he was not uninitiated to the spy craft. In the given premise, it was an ingenious idea. Besides, it came from Amjad. 'I hope I don't regret trusting you. We'll get some classified documents onsite, create a fake trail. Make it a scene of encounter. Delhi Police observed Radha based on the trail of these documents which led to the file he died with. They'll take some time to realize the story is fake, and you'll be ahead till that time.'

'Don't forget to put it on Doordarshan.' Amjad smiled.

Sonia was amazed at Amjad's maneuvering—or, as some would say, manipulation. Amjad had gotten out of the mess by settling a favor while sending the terrorists on a wild goose chase.

'Search his house. Track down the device he used to communicate and get it in your custody before the Delhi Police arrives.'

The MARCOS left the mall duly to complete his command.

After covering all the traces, Amjad tapped Sonia's shoulder. 'Good job.'

Sonia was feeling so confident that she decided to ask the question she'd had for a while directly to Amjad. 'Would you mind if I ask you something?'

'Shoot.'

'If I'm so good, why have neither you nor Abhimanyu sent me on mission yet?'

Amjad was surprised. 'You *are* on a mission.'

'Field mission, I mean.'

Amjad looked into her confident eyes and knew she wouldn't be satisfied with anything less. But it was a risk he was not yet ready to take. 'You should bide your time and increase your strength while you can.'

Sonia wouldn't take no for an answer this time. 'For how long?'

Amjad was in a spot. He nodded but muttered, 'Be careful what you wish for,' and exited the van.

Sonia found it strange, for these were also Abhimanyu's lines. What frightened them was still beyond her fancy.

'Come on, let's go. We have a broken arrow and a safehouse to fix.'

Sonia followed him quietly. She was disappointed but also curious at his response.

Arup's men may have zeroed in on the truck location by now, but he was anxious to get an update for Bagyidaw's, since it had gone eerily silent. They were greeted with dead silence as they entered the control room. Tensed faces doted the walls. Arup saw them first. 'We were looking for you.'

'Ah, we just had to finish an internal call.'

Arup could spot the bluff, but he had something more acute at his hands now.

A young analyst ran to Amjad with a paper in hand. 'Sir.' He handed him the latest dossier.

Amjad's eye had caught the mayhem by now. The big screen was telling an unbelievable story. Arup's unit had reached the Bagyidaw's bungalow, and they were getting the live feed. 'Start from the door again.'

Dead bodies lay at the entrance. The MARCOS Amjad had sent couldn't even make it to the door. Their bodies lay dead outside the vehicles at the gate. It had been an ambush. Terrorists had reached the bungalow before them. As the camera moved inside, it revealed more bodies. More commandos lay dead across the house, hit with one or two bullets in the head. There was no sign of struggle, as if everyone had been caught by surprise. Amjad couldn't explain it. No one could. The morbid scenes were beyond belief. Blood spatter blotched the walls, floors, and curtains. The dead faces with their open eyes told a petrifying story of horror that incited more fear.

Amjad mustered some courage to ask the question that bothered him most. 'Where is Thapa, Sasha?' He expected to be hurt.

The commandos searched for him throughout the bungalow, room by room. They eventually found him in the communication room next to the satellite links.

'He died trying to communicate with us,' Arup said, his voice hoarse.

Thapa had been shot point blank, and his body was mutilated beyond recognition. A large paper was stuck to his chest: *Tell him we have her*. This was beyond Amjad's worst fears. A dead Sasha was better than this situation. The terrorists had Abhimanyu's identity. They had Sasha, and they had the nuke. The frightening truth paralyzed him for a moment. Abhimanyu was more than just his protégé—he was a son to him—and his life was unraveling right in front of his eyes. Amjad also knew from experience that terrorists never leave such high-value targets alive. Her name was just a bargaining chip for them, but carrying her around would be foolhardy, for they had a bigger mission. She was probably already dead.

It took some time for Amjad to feel Arup's hand on his shoulder. He looked at the paper Arup held. 'Last time my men caught a frequency, it was a few kilometers from the Bagyidaw's bungalow.' Amjad signaled a teary-eyed Sonia to zoom out the area on the big screen. 'Blow it up.' Anything would have been better than the scenes from Bagyidaw's bungalow. 'They must still be in the area,' Amjad said, his voice still low.

'This is the closest we've been to them.'

All was still not lost. Most importantly, the focus had to be on guiding another MARCOS team to the nuke now. Arup tried to pull back the spirits.

Amjad was beginning to think again. He wondered about the terrorists' real motives behind capturing Sasha. This couldn't have been a part of the original plan. It would have been pointless. But now, it suited them, because Abhimanyu was leading a mission and had been successful to stop the first team. They had to neutralize him, so they had to divert from their original plan. The terrorists had been pushed from their holes and their comfort zones. Abhimanyu was their boogeyman now.

Abhimanyu had been there earlier and had done it in Chennai. He was also the best shot Indians had in this moment. Amjad's paternal protective instincts clashed against his professional judgement. The terrorists needed Abhimanyu to be off the case immediately and decided to open a personal front for him. So, Amjad decided to do exactly the opposite of what was anticipated of him.

'They wanted to distract us by attacking Bagyidaw's, but in doing so, they revealed their location. It's a foolish bargain,' Arup said.

'They knew the risks, but they still did it. They are desperate. Just in case Sasha is still alive, they'll have her. Who better than Abhimanyu to save her?'

Sonia couldn't believe her ears, but Amjad had firmed up in his mind. She knew Amjad's coldhearted reasons.

'You want Abhimanyu to do this. Aare you sure?'

'Yes.'

'Amjad, we may risk the success of our entire mission on the emotional stability of one person.' Arup made no pretentions of his apprehensions. After all, everyone had a breaking point.

'Think rationally, Arup. Abhimanyu is our best bet, for he is the only one amongst all of us who was there in Chennai, there at the Teesta bridge, and knows them the best. Abhimanyu has been in this situation, and besides, he's also the one nearest to the location. And time is precious.'

'Amjad, any man's fortitude can break on hearing this kind of news.'

'His shouldn't.'

'Why?'

'It's a test of his training. The division spends a fortune to train them for moments like these. Now we need to trust his instincts.'

'Which division?'

'Special Activities Division, RAW,' Amjad said very slowly.

Arup was quiet for a moment; he had a sudden realization. 'So, it's true. That's what they call it.'

Amjad nodded.

Arup had nothing more to ask. He had heard stories of an unknown entity managing psywar and psyops within RAW—commandos going berserk and killing their own ministers, corporate honchos taking decisions to hemorrhage their own companies but eventually helping the country, villages losing memories overnight; the stories were many and most of them very unrealistic, relegated to myth. But people on the frontline knew something such as this existed. They just didn't know where. No wonder the same division had trained the MARCOS to control their emotions under extremely torturous conditions.

Amjad dialed in Abhimanyu. 'Alpha India, come in?'

'Alpha India online.'

'Get Akram on the same line.' Despite the training, Amjad needed insurance against Abhimanyu's reactions.

This was a different ballgame, and they couldn't afford anything foolish.

'Akram, patched in.'

'We have something to share with you, Abhimanyu. Before that, we need you to be calm. We can't afford an unconstrained reaction from you.'

Abhimanyu was surprised then scared, for he quickly imagined it had to do something with Sasha.

'Sasha has been kidnapped, and our intelligence suggests she is with the terrorists who are also carrying the nuke.' Akram immediately grasped his role and reached for Abhimanyu.

Abhimanyu was numb, but he had the sense to switch to autopilot immediately. He felt Akram's hand on his shoulder.

'They want to use it as a leverage against you, against us. I don't want to give it to them, so you need to finish the mission for us and save Sasha as well. Nobody can do it better than you. But for that, you'll need to keep yourself together. Can you do that?' Amjad had offloaded all he could. He had created an emotional surge with a rational proposition for Abhimanyu.

Abhimanyu, dazed at what he had heard, just inhaled to digest everything and keep his perspective.

'Abhimanyu, do you copy? Can you do this?'

The pressure was debilitating, and Abhimanyu wasn't ready for it.

Akram realized Abhimanyu was tuning out. He had to make a choice now. Akram switched off the coms. 'Alpha India, come in. Alpha India, come in.'

'He has cut the line.'

Arup was aghast.

'Hey, hey, you need to tell them you can still do it.'

Abhimanyu was hit emotionally. The commandos were here for this mission, so he needed to understand they were here for him and Sasha as well.

'We are with you,' Akram emphasized.

Even Abhimanyu was unsure if he was fit enough for the mission now. 'But—'

'There is no other choice, Abhimanyu.' Akram gripped his hand, shook him a bit and interrupted before Abhimanyu could say anything.

Akram's persuasion finally moved the needle. Abhimanyu regained his composure and the realization they had no choice. The road to save Sasha and the road to neutralize the terrorists was the same. There was just more at stake now for him personally. Fate had been kind enough to give him a second chance with Sasha, and he wouldn't lose it without a fight. They had to bite the bullet and chew the steel away. No second option existed, no second life. He switched on the coms. 'We'll do it.'

Amjad closed his fist. 'I knew you wouldn't disappoint.'

Of course, Abhimanyu had a choice—a choice to walk away from all of it, or even to just refocus on Sasha only. A true soldier or a spy was made in such pressure moments when they had everything on the line. Abhimanyu had proven his worth just by making this choice. Amjad couldn't express his contentment.

'So, let us revise the basics. We need to ensure all bases are covered. We locate them in the area, move in silently on them, shoot or sedate them, vacuum wrap the bomb, find Sasha and get out.'

'You have their latest location?'

'On your screen,' Sonia said. 'Their location hasn't changed in the last two rounds, but we are still to get an accurate fix on it. Its accuracy is to a mile right now.'

'We should move in then,' Abhimanyu said, realizing the terrorists were moving toward them.

'You're the closest airborne team, but don't engage till the backup arrives. Once all of you are in place, have everyone in sight, and everything as per the plan, only then can you move in.'

'How much time for the backup to arrive?'

'The closest MARCOS backup is sixty minutes behind you.'

'We can't wait sixty minutes, Amjad. The backups can join us when they arrive.'

'You're missing the point, Abhimanyu. These are professionals. They've beaten the communication systems at the Bagyidaw's, managed to deceive Thapa's local intelligence network, even kill two MARCOS teams and many army commandos. They have the brains and numbers too—could easily be ten to fifteen. You need a comprehensive plan with more men and more ammunition.'

'With due respect, sir, we have the surprise element right now. If you trust Rupesh, the timer will be out soon. Right now, they're on the move, and once they're settled in, they'll only be more careful in guarding the spot. It'll get tougher to penetrate their security. Even if we do penetrate, they'll definitely set a trap on the bombs. We'll be cutting it too close. We can't risk this wait.' Abhimanyu was relentless and willing to risk it all now. Perhaps he had too much on the line, and that, by itself, made Abhimanyu cold to all risk; akin to gambling, he was on the tilt.

'Abhimanyu, we'll stick to the plan. Consider it an order.' But before Amjad could finish, the line disconnected.

'Are you with me?'

Akram and Siddhartha agreed with Abhimanyu. They believed they could do it. In the forces, hierarchy was clear, but on the field, the commander's word was the final gospel. Everything else was noise. Akram agreed the advantages of the surprise element and extra time would work in their favor. After all, these elements had also helped them at the Teesta bridge. He was the most experienced MARCO on the team and decided to stand by his commander.

'We'll get her, and the nuke.'

The others nodded to Akram.

Abhimanyu felt more confident now.

'I told you not to trust him. He has too much baggage to handle.' Arup was in despair.

Amjad couldn't help but wonder if the advantage he had thought he had in Abhimanyu would soon turn into a handicap. 'Keep trying to connect,' he told Sonia.

CHAPTER 20

THE TURN

Ghatakpunji, Assam

It was two hours past midnight. Abhimanyu maintained low altitude to have higher ground visibility. They reached the tagged location only to find no one there anymore. After scouting the ground from different angles, he soft landed his MI-35M on a small piece of flat rocky land just outside the town of Ghatakpunji. Abhimanyu, Akram, and two army commandoes—Lieutenant Abhishek and Lieutenant Shikhar—walked into the village in single file. Siddhartha and the third army commando stayed back to guard the Mi-35M along with the backup pilot.

They entered the village in two groups and rendezvoused in the center of town under a gigantic fig tree the village men held sacred—popularly known as the peepal in India—located on raised ground. It was half past two, and the entire village was in a deep slumber. With no one there, the MARCOS could use it as a good vantage point.

Abhimanyu opened the map on his wrist tab. 'We're within fifty meters from the source point. Signal seems to be weak, and it's hard to get the exact direction right.'

'We came in from south, so that's ruled out,' Shikhar said.

'Most residences are in the west. I doubt they'd setup the base in the main village,' Akram added.

'That leaves us with the east and north directions.' Abhimanyu handed him the gear and climbed the peepal tree. He reached the top and could even see the chopper now. 'I can see some lights.' Abhimanyu pointed eastward. Darkness had covered the valley, but two lights flickered oddly at this hour, accentuated against the dark canvass of a peaceful night.

'Around sixty meters from us,' Akram said. 'They could just be villagers.'

'Let's check it out. See who they are. If they are villagers, why are they still awake?'

The roads were deserted, and the eastern part of the village was largely uninhabited. containing the school, the post office, and a pond. With hardly any manmade cover, they used the cover of trees to move from block to block in a column. A watchman manned the school, but he was asleep. The post office was locked. The MARCOS kept moving through the night fog till Akram raised his palm, pointing back at shoulder height. They stopped. He had heard a sound. Akram signaled toward its source. Gradually, others could hear a very faint but consistent chatter. They had to rely on hand gestures now.

One by one, they moved into the dark spot behind the hut and finally stopped at the sight of a young kid few meters ahead on top of a small rock. He could not be more than twenty years old, but he looked serious. His right hand was hidden on his backside and not moving. The kid surely had something in his hand on the far side, which was hard to spot even with the night vision.

Shikhar had spotted him. With his palms down at shoulder height, Shikhar signaled at the kid.

The killed raised his right hand.

Shikhar saw him holding a semi-automatic rifle. He raised his left hand, forefinger and thumb extended.

Abhimanyu signaled everyone to lay low, and everyone went on one knee. They quietly checked their gun locks and accessories.

There was more movement. The kid was still alert. Most movement was closer to another hut which was farther away.

Akram leaned toward the right to have a better view through his night binoculars. They were at the right place. He signaled with an open fist, which meant he could see around ten men inside. Akram readjusted the binoculars' lens, and, for a moment, he couldn't believe his eyes. He pointed toward it and signaled a mushroom cloud with fingers.

That was it; no one could confuse it. They had spotted the miniaturized nuke and out of its armory—a naked nuke. Beside it was a computerized circuit to trigger the nuke. They had seen it earlier in their careers and were witnessing it again—only bigger and deadlier this time.

Abhimanyu followed in and tried to locate any markings with his binoculars. It was marked two hundred KVT—much higher than the last one in Chennai, which was only a forty KVT. It was perplexing to imagine how the terrorists managed to procure such a high-grade weapon. This was not just a Pakistani conspiracy. They didn't have such high-grade nukes.

The men moving around it seemed to be in rush to do something. Abhimanyu wasn't an expert, but it only took common sense to guess the terrorists were preparing for detonation.

Akram slowly removed his compact bandoleer—designed by DRDO and carried five hundred bullets in one load—from the bag and readied himself for the showdown.

Abhishek and Shikhar checked their grenades, smoke bombs, and magazines.

It was time to bring in the cavalry, so Abhimanyu activated his communications on the wrist pad. *Delta, come in. Delta, come in.*

Alpha India, copy that. Explain your location.

On the hot seat.

Amjad couldn't believe his eyes. His boys had it in sight and were ready to attack.

Reconfirm the sighting.

Alpha India on hot seat. Repeat, Alpha India on hot seat. Abhimanyu clicked a photo with his binoculars and relayed it back.

Sonia ran the check on the device—a positive match. It was a naked nuke close to detonation. 'They are ready to detonate,' she said in shock, looking at Amjad. The satellites had been refocused and were tracking the inbound and outbound routes now. The hut appeared on the big screen.

'Sasha?' Amjad asked.

'No trace yet,' Akram replied.

'Extraction team is on its way to check the inbound and outbound routes.'

Abhimanyu had to take his mind off it. If the terrorists had to use her, they would show their hand sooner than later. It was a risky and farfetched bet, but, in that moment, it was a logical thought to Abhimanyu, and even to Amjad who could half-guess Abhimanyu's game plan. He had to just keep his eyes open for her and press the trigger at the right target.

The terrorists were busy in the motions of the final setup. Abhimanyu realized this was the perfect moment to catch them by surprise. Abhimanyu did not want to wait for the reinforcements. 'Permission to initiate the hot pursuit.'

Amjad was not surprised at hearing it, unlike Arup. The Indians didn't know the time of detonation, but everything looked set, so it was at the terrorists' discretion. Besides, Amjad also realized the terrorists would notice the arrival of a larger contingent in such narrow passages around the hut. The backup would only alert the terrorists. The drone footage on the screen called for immediate action.

Amjad checked his watch to see it was three thirty in the morning. The sun rose early in this part of the world, and darkness wouldn't be their ally for long. The village had slept, the nearest reinforcements were at least thirty minutes away, and time was quickly running out. The surprise factor would only work if they moved in now. He would be risking their lives, but the odds would deteriorate quickly with time. Amjad decided to take the plunge. 'Permission granted. Make it quick. I want to have my breakfast with you on time.'

Abhimanyu smiled. The team split into two. Akram moved in with Shikhar to the right while Abhimanyu moved in with Abhishek to the left. Abhimanyu signaled Akram to take the first shot at the man handling the nuke and kill the rest thereafter. They were moving toward the front, and Shikhar got ready to provide sniper cover. He signaled Abhishek to move behind the nearby tanker with him and provide cover when he moved toward the nuke. Abhimanyu aimed to vacuum wrap the nuke in a sheet of alloy DRDO had designed block signals and cut off the circuitry. That would avoid detonation. He signaled with round fingers through his eyes to Abhishek, telling him to provide sniper cover. With a V sign to his nose, he asked if anyone had any doubt.

Everyone answered with a thumbs up, except Abhishek. He rotated up his magazine and pointed it skyward. Abhishek was asking if the terrorists had any heavy fire, in which case, just the four of them wouldn't be enough to take on the terrorists.

Abhimanyu pointed to the naked nuke and then to the sentry carrying only a semi-automatic. It didn't make sense for them to carry heavy fire. It added too much load and couldn't be used around a live nuke either. This would be a close combat. Abhimanyu signaled at the pistol and the knives.

Abhishek gave him a thumbs up and got ready.

Abhimanyu then signaled again at Shikhar and Abhishek with the sniper sign. The two of them had to take out as many terrorists as possible in the first hit itself. One didn't want too many hands to fight later. Finally, Abhimanyu raised his left hand with closed fist and moved it back and forward—the call sign to start.

Abhimanyu and Abhishek moved toward the tanker. They had to retire the sentry first. Abhimanyu removed the chloroform spray from his tracks, sprayed it on a few tissues from his side pocket and signaled Abhishek to be ready to shoot with a silencer if needed.

It wasn't needed. The spotter was looking through his binoculars to the area where their chopper had landed.

Abhimanyu wondered what had exactly attracted his attention toward the chopper. He moved in quickly from the dark right and incapacitated him.

The spotter was unconscious within seconds and fell down the edge of the knife. His throat was slit without a whisper.

Abhimanyu used his binoculars to look for himself. He was surprised to see three people approximately a hundred meters from the helicopter. They could just be the local police or villagers, but it made him anxious.

Meanwhile, Akram and Shikhar had reached their spot, and they couldn't hide there for long. They did not have much time, and the window to take a clear shot would be lost if they were discovered.

Abhimanyu signaled the others to be aware of the movement around the helicopter and took his position next to the tanker. The MARCOS were all set. Abhimanyu focused on the nuke through his rifle's scope and waited for an opening. This could finally be it—the end of a mission that nearly got them captured in New York, killed across the Rajasthan border, and still had him with his family on the line. The only other question was, where was Sasha?

A shot thundered through the door, interrupting his thoughts. The man next to the nuke was down. Terrorists ran toward their semi-automatics. Some randomly shot with handguns. This was it. The MARCOS had taken the terrorists by surprise, and they didn't know where the shot had come from.

Akram took aim and fired his automatic rifle at three hundred rounds per minute. The ten-millimeter rounds could pierce the walls and still hit the targets.

Shikhar took position about twenty meters from Akram, where he had a clear sight of both the windows and the back door. Shikhar picked off anyone who exited this door and window one at a time.

Finally, Akram could count eight dead terrorists in the hut—five kills to him and the rest to Shikhar as they had tried to escape. The hut was silenced without movement or noise for several seconds.

Akram signaled to Abhimanyu, and he took the run to the hut. Bodies laid around in a pool of blood. Two of them were wired with suicide vests. They couldn't have risked it near the nuke anyway. It was their exit plan. Taken by surprise, they had no time to act.

Abhimanyu checked the corners, dark spots, and other usual hiding spots. It was all clear. Then he heard some movement from the second hut and immediately signaled to the others.

Shikhar signaled back with his palm over the left eye, rifle in the right. He had his eyes on the movement. He could see more people inside the safehouse.

Akram turned to his right to guard the hut from that end, and Abhishek guarded the entry point to the area.

They had the hut surrounded, and Abhimanyu had to quickly deactivate the nuke inside. All the effort put into infiltrating Pakistan to get Khalid and the hard disk had prepared them for this moment. If the retina scan and fingerprints matched, it shouldn't take time. He patched in the control room with his tab and attached it to the nuke's explosive discharge circuitry.

Sonia took control from here. She was on it in a flash as Amjad watched over her in the Guwahati control room.

He was anxious for the crack team to leave the area and still nervous about Sasha's whereabouts. He knew he would soon have to go all in with Abhimanyu's team. The drones had just reached the area, and Amjad had the visuals now. The huts were visible, thanks to the lights, but Amjad thought he saw some movement near the helicopters. It was impossible to see anything in this darkness without a local source of light. They could only see dark shadows perhaps interacting with the pilot and the commandos. Amjad got curious. 'Can you connect us to the chopper?'

'Coms are down. I don't know why.'

A technical glitch was highly unlikely for a fully serviced MI-35M. They could be just locals, but he needed more confirmation to have a closure on it as soon as possible.

Akram saw some movement inside the hut and soon heard a shot.

Shikhar, who had the direct view of the second hut, had been shot in head. It looked like a sniper shot from the hut.

'Man down. I repeat, man down.' Akram broke radio silence and unloaded his Negev recoilless automatic light machinegun with enough firepower to penetrate the hut walls and drag out whoever was inside. Shadows moved in a frenzy inside the hut, and he just followed them till it came to a halt. Amjad had fired more than a hundred bullets in those thirty seconds. He saw two men exiting slowly with their hands raised. The night fog made it difficult to have a clear view of their faces outside the hut light.

'Stop!' Abhimanyu roared.

Another slender figure emerged from hut with raised hands. The three of them kneeled with hands still up.

Akram had to see their faces. Abhimanyu gave him the cover while he carefully approached them. The Negev automatic was back on his shoulders, and the semi-automatic Glock 19 and Glock 26 pistols were in both hands, pointed at the three of them. 'Keep your heads down. Hands in the air or I'll shoot through your heads. Bury you into the ground right here.'

Abhimanyu quickly moved into the hut with the nuke, leaving Abhishek behind to cover Akram.

In the control room, people could only watch the flashes of firing near the huts. They had their heart in their mouth. A naked nuke lay right there.

Akram spoke into the coms, slowly, 'How much more time you need to deactivate it?'

'Five minutes.'

'Make it quick. We don't know how many more of them are here.'

'Certainly many more than we thought.' Abhimanyu was nervous, but he refocused on securing the nuke.

Amjad and Arup watched Sonia in despair as she worked on the code to break the encryption and gain access. An entire team at the Tunnel was helping her with it.

Thanks to the fog, the terrorists' faces were still not visible.

Akram walked closer to the hostages but maintained a distance of ten meters. The margins were very thin here. Abhishek gave him cover, but he was stretched by the double task of protecting him and keeping a lookout at the entrance as well. It was hard to verify their identities through the cameras in Abhishek's rifle scopes, as he was quite far. The drones wouldn't give a clear picture to the control room either. Thankfully, the Glock 26 came with a low-caliber camera retrofitted for face recognition.

Even though Amjad couldn't see their faces, the camera picked up enough once Akram pointed it toward each of them. The feed went to their night vision cameras and the command center. The first man, Mou-ul-Ghir, was a terrorist who had been captured a year ago in Assam. But he had escaped a few months ago from the central prison in Guwahati. The second was Rouhani Aslam, known to be active in Afghanistan till last year. These were amongst the most infamous terrorists known to the intelligence agencies clearly handpicked for this mission. However, the system didn't turn up anything for the third one.

Akram moved closer to look at him. It was not a him; it was a her. 'Third suspect is a woman,' he said into the coms and faced her. 'Show me your face!' Akram's Glock 19 was still aimed at the other two terrorists while his Glock 26 trained at her head.

The female's hand moved behind her in a sharp movement.

Akram was alarmed. 'Don't move your hand!'

Her hand stopped by the waist.

'Show me your face, or I'll shoot you! Now!' he shouted with extreme aggression.

When she looked up, Akram couldn't believe what he saw. It was a face he knew too well. It was a face Abhimanyu knew too well. It was a face Amjad knew too well. They didn't need to run an ID on it. It was one of their own—Sasha.

Akram was taken aback, and the command center had a pin-drop silence.

Amjad couldn't comprehend why was she not being used as a bargaining chip if she was a hostage.

Akram pulled himself together. 'Sasha, is that you? Are you a hostage?'

Sasha unsheathed a knife from her waist and stabbed Akram.

Akram couldn't comprehend what was happening.

Seizing the moment, Mou took Akram's Glock 19, pointed it at his face and shot Akram through his head.

'I was a hostage. Now I'm free.'

Rouhani took Akram's automatic gun along with his bandoleer, which still had at least a hundred bullets left—good enough for one strong burst.

The two men rose and ran toward the hut.

Amjad couldn't see much but had heard enough. A teary-eyed Amjad tried to put everything into perspective as quickly as he could. While still coming to terms with everything he had heard, Amjad shouted, 'Abhimanyu, incoming! Code red! I repeat, code red!' Sasha had killed Akram. She was not a hostage. She was with the terrorists. Only time would answer why. For now, he had to get out of this situation.

Abhishek ran toward Abhimanyu and took position just as Mou and Rouhani entered the hut.

'How much more time?' Amjad asked Sonia.

Sonia gathered herself even as tears rolled down her cheeks. 'Almost there. Thirty seconds more.'

Meanwhile, Abhimanyu was solely focused on vacuum wrapping the bomb after connecting the pads. With bullets flying around, it would prevent the bomb from any external damage. Unaware of what had transpired outside, Abhimanyu only came to his senses when he heard Amjad calling a code red. That was unlike Amjad's calm demeanor. Something had snapped. Abhimanyu turned and heard footsteps rushing toward him—obviously not friends. His job with the bomb was done. He had to protect it now. He unholstered his Beretta 92FS automatic pistol and Glock 26 in other hand. 'Akram, Abhishek, cover me.' Abhimanyu shot at the moving figures as they passed across the window. They were fast; he missed. Abhimanyu was surprised and prepared for them to turn up at the door, but they didn't.

'Automatic fire, coming your away.' Abhishek tried to give him a heads up.

Rouhani fired at Abhishek and pinned him to his spot. He couldn't look up again.

Before Abhimanyu could react, Mou shot with Akram's Negev through the walls. With such heavy incoming fire, Abhimanyu pulled back behind a pillar. Mou kept firing till he ran out of bullets.

'Damn it, Abhishek. What are you doing? Where are you, Akram? I need support. These guys have gone mad. They're shooting at a live nuke inside.' Abhimanyu barely saved himself but was taken aback by terrorist's firepower. A bullet shell landed next to him, dead from the recoil from the wall. He picked it up and realized it was a MARCOS bullet.

'Listen carefully, Abhimanyu. Akram is down. I repeat, Akram is down,' Amjad said again.

Abhimanyu inspected the bullet again and recognized it from Akram's IMI Negev. At first, he was hurt. Then he was angry. How could they have gotten the better of AKram? Abhimanyu noticed that even with the Negev, the terrorists hadn't fired anywhere close to the nuke. They were very well trained indeed.

Mou fired again with his own Ak-56.

Abhimanyu was now furious. He pulled his M4A1 assault rifle from his shoulder and fired back.

Rouhani and Mou retreated due to the heavy fire, giving Abhishek an opportunity to move out of his pit again.

He sniped at them, but they were good; they moved behind the trees in no time. Abhimanyu was at the door and out for vengeance. He fired at the trees, but the terrorists were moving fast.

Abhishek kept sniping at every opportunity but to no avail.

Finally, Abhimanyu ran out of magazine clips and took cover behind the wall.

Once Abhishek ran out of his load, a grave silence engulfed the encounter site.

With no incoming fire, the terrorists unloaded, breaking the silence—but not at both of them, only at Abhishek. They had to take out the sniper.

Abhimanyu was, by now, not surprised by their awareness. These were hard-trained militias, probably as well trained as themselves. If not for the initial ambush, the four of them stood no chance against these men. The surprise had made all the difference.

'I'm hit,' Abhishek said into the coms after a bullet grazed his right shoulder.

Abhimanyu realized the situation was dire. 'Put on the masks.' He removed the alpha-grade tranquilizer and rolled it toward the two of them.

Both the terrorists jumped away from the can, but it wasn't a bomb.

Abhishek shot the can, and, in no time, there was a pin-drop silence. One can had enough to sleep induce an entire village.

'You'll have a lot of cleanup to do,' Abhimanyu said.

Amjad didn't respond, for he had bigger concerns.

'It's done.' Sonia looked at Amjad. They had deactivated the circuitry. Now they just needed to take it to a safe place. But it was impossible for just Abhimanyu and Abhishek to carry it all the way to the helicopter. The backup was only a few minutes away.

Amjad considered the possibilities. The bomb was dead, terrorists were killed, but a wild card was still out in the open—Sasha. It was dangerous for them to stay there. His prime concern now was to get his men out alive. 'Air wrap the bomb with concrete and move out of there now.'

Abhimanyu retrieved a seemingly innocuous white bag. The bag was bulletproof, not that anyone would risk firing bullets on a nuke. More importantly, no one could move it once settled. Abhimanyu air wrapped the nuke with four holes into the concrete, one at each corner, while Abhishek kept a lookout; he knew a third terrorist was still missing. 'Any ID on the woman?' Abhimanyu asked.

Sonia and Arup eyed Amjad. Should they or should they not tell him? 'No, not yet.' They had achieved the mission's objective, and Amjad's main focus was to just get them out safely now. The backups would deal with Sasha later. She couldn't escape from these jungles anyway.

With all set, Abhimanyu moved backward and entered a code on his pad. The film straightened, held at the corners. Even a tank couldn't move the rigid wall that had erected. The mission was a success, but Abhimanyu felt dejected, for he had lost a comrade.

'Let's move. Quick,' Abhishek said nervously.

'Wait.' Abhimanyu approached the trees where Mou and Rouhani lay unconscious. He unholstered his Glock and fired a shot into their foreheads without remorse.

'Abhimanyu, evidence?' Abhishek asked with his coms off.

'I don't care. We have two less scoundrels in this world.' The emotions had gotten the better of him. 'But, where's the third one?'

Abhishek shrugged. 'Maybe … escaped toward the hills.'

'She won't go far.' Abhimanyu knew a cavalry was coming her way.

'Okay, let's move,' Amjad said again.

Abhimanyu and Abhishek approached the helicopter through the haze of a chloroform derivative.

'Keep your head in. Just a few more minutes,' Amjad cautioned them without sharing the details yet. What was

Sasha scheming? Where had she disappeared? The nuke was dead and diffused. She would be trying to escape. However, she probably knew she couldn't stay hidden in the valley for long. Neither could she outsmart the hordes of search parties who'll blanket the hills to hunt her down. How would she escape?

They approached the helicopter unaware of the threat looming in the open. But, as they got closer, an eerie silence greeted them. The third army commando—the spotter—was missing. Weirdly enough, the copter's taxi lights were also off.

Abhimanyu stealthily walked up to the copter from the side with his M4A1 aimed at it.

Abhishek approached it from the rear. To his shock, the pilots were dead. The pilots' bodies were stacked up in the back seat, but someone remained in the pilot's seat. Abhishek signaled to Abhimanyu with a neck cut that the pilots were dead and, with the left hand over his left eye, signaling someone else was inside.

In an instant, Abhimanyu switched to his Glock in the right and a grenade in the left hand. 'Who's in there?' Abhimanyu shouted with his guns pointed at the back of the pilot's seat.

It was a woman; perhaps the same one from the huts, he thought. She turned around. A known face. His first expression was of happiness, a smile. Then confusion. Was she a hostage? Was she running away? Was she forced? Whatever it was, she was alive. He smiled at her, watching the bloodstained knife in her hands. So, that's how she saved herself, he thought.

'Yes, it's me.' Sasha discarded the knife toward the dead pilots and produced a gun.

Abhimanyu's eyes followed the knife and then the wound on the pilots chest. They had been killed by the same knife. He realized she had perhaps killed the pilots. It was too late.

Sasha pulled the trigger. 'Sorry, honey,' she said as he fell to the edge of the helicopter.

He tried to stand. 'Why?'.

She shot again.

Abhimanyu went silent.

She took out Abhimanyu's tab.

Amjad couldn't see much, but the sound was clear through the coms. The command center had plunged into deeper despair now. The mission was still extracting expensive sacrifice, one at a time. 'Abhishek, hold back. Hide!'

'But—'

'Do as I say. Take cover and make sure you have a clear shot at the chopper. The reinforcements will arrive shortly. You need to hold her from flying out till then.'

Abhishek moved from the back side of the helicopter. Thankfully, the helicopter between them covered him.

Amjad had grasped Sasha's escape plan. 'If she does, we'll lose her forever. It's very hard for even the best of the radars to track that stealth machine in those hills, and we must assume she knows how to fly it by now.'

Abhishek searched for a vantage point. He crawled back and slowly climbed a rock about thirty meters from the chopper. He prepared his suppressed sniper rifle—a VSS Vintorez—and aimed for the rotors.

Arup wondered where she would go and how far. 'What is she trying to do?'

Amjad realized Sasha wasn't far from the Bangladesh border. 'Sonia, how far is the Bangladesh border?'

'Eighty kilometers.'

'In that chopper, its barely fifteen minutes, and once it lifts off, we won't be able to track it easily.'

Arup had his answer. They needed everything now. He called the Indian Air Force Chief.

Meanwhile, Sasha pulled off Abhimanyu's backpack and removed the transistor that connected the pad to the satellites. She snatched his wrist pad too. The embedded communication protocols and encryptions the Indians used were now available to her. It wouldn't help her reactivate the bomb, but in the right hands, the analysis could help them unlock a lot of gateways. Sasha got into the co-pilot's seat. Someone else was with her too, but Abhishek couldn't get a view. The cockpit lights went on, and the camera in the rifle's scope immediately identified them—Rasheesh Kamble, another former Indian intelligence operative.

Amjad knew the helicopter very well, as he had flown it. 'Hit the rotors as soon as they are of the ground.' Once airborne, the pilots would be focused on keeping the rotors aligned. It would give Abhishek just enough time to take a few clear shots, especially from the back, given the pilots were blindsided. Hitting the rotor engine would be very difficult, as the MI-35M accelerated quickly, and on the ground, Sasha and Rasheesh had the numerical advantage over Abhishek. Take off was the best moment for Abhishek strike.

Abhishek scanned the nearby forests with his night visions but found no movement. However, he noticed someone hiding behind the trees left to his spot. He slowly approached with his Glock at the high ready. Whoever it was, he was very calm, for he didn't react even when Abhishek had reached the other side of the tree. With a side swing, Abhishek turned straight in front him, pistol on his temple. It was Siddhartha. He was dead and so were three others next to him.

The third army commando, Maheshwar, was amongst them. The other two were perhaps terrorists. Sasha and Rasheesh had hidden their bodies to avoid any suspicion. He checked Siddhartha pulse; he was still alive but barely. Abhishek took his body to the side and gave him a few injections of IV, for his body would need to survive till help arrived. He heard the rotors.

'Abhishek, shoot,' Amjad said.

With the choppers lights on, the drone could spot it, and the command center had a clear view on the screen. The chopper was taking off. Abhishek ran to the rock and took position, but it was perhaps too late. The chopper had gained speed. Abhishek's bullets missed the rotor and only managed to hit the metal chassis but to no avail.

'Someone is still alive and hiding in the forest.' Sasha smiled.

'We should take him out then.' Rasheesh turned around the chopper.

Abhishek saw it and ran for cover, for he would be no match for MI-35M's guns.

'No, I think we should just go,' Sasha said.

Rasheesh was halfway through the turn but abandoned the idea at Sasha's behest. He turned it back, but it was too late. Sasha saw bright lights approaching in the horizon—the Indian reinforcements. Rasheesh took the helicopter straight up with great thrust and quickly gained height over the reinforcements. It would be an easy escape from here, he thought, unaware that a Mirage 2000 already diving down and had him on its lock screen. The Mirage hit them with its 30mm cannon gun, and the tail rotor immediately went out of control. The rogue helicopter crashed downward. Thankfully, the fuel tanks were still intact.

Abhishek ran toward the wreckage and pulled out Sasha and Rasheesh. They were unconscious but alive.

The Indian helicopters had them encircled. One by one, they landed around the crash site, and the commando force of the Indian Air Force—the Garuds—secured the perimeter.

Sasha had gained partial consciousness and knew she was hit. She could barely see anything in the dark sky.

Abhishek gave Sasha and Rashesh an anesthesia, and the Garuds loaded them into their helicopters.

Meanwhile, another set of helicopters rushed Abhimanyu, Siddhartha, and Abhishek to the military Hospital.

CHAPTER 21

THE HAND

Bagyidaw's Bungalow, January 23

Four Hours Ago

It was late at night, and the nocturnal animals of the jungle were busy with their hunting tasks. The prey looked for a place far from the hunters, but no place was far enough to hide from the shadow of night. The hunters were tasked with finding chinks in their safety armor. They did it by exploring all the likely locations one by one. The deadliest hunters, however, were the ones who used camouflaged. They had hidden themselves not today but a day earlier, or sometimes even before that. The deadly Indian python was one such predator. It hid for hours and sometimes even days in such corners and waited for its prey to come to him. Not surprisingly, the python managed to kill animals much larger than itself. It struck at the most unexpected time in the safest of corners. The strike was lethal enough to choke even the strongest of cats.

In nature's balancing act, if the python got its mark wrong, these very cats could still tear it apart. But it seldom got it wrong, because the python had mastered the art of exploiting the vulnerable moments. It quietly curled around the neck and the upper spinal cord of the big cats when they were asleep. It tightened the noose very slowly, and by the time the cats realized it, it was too late. The more they tried, the heavier they breathed and the more they got asphyxiated. If they tried to use their weight and move, the python's hold would transfer all the force on the spine. The python itself had no bones and could squeeze endlessly till its prey's spine would break and give way. The cat's strengths had made it fallible now. The night had turned the hunter into a prey, thanks to the wild card—Python.

Her wait was finally over today. The device Sasha had hidden in the teak house was finally beeping. Like a python, she had stayed hidden for a long time—over a decade. Scanning the jungle, she reveled in the quietness of night. The days of being hunted for the mole that she was would end today. She had patiently waited for it, and now she had to deliver the final blow that would break the enemy's back. Sasha took her silencer—a Sig Saur SRD9, the latest one available—and fit it into the Glock 19 she had commandeered from the safehouse's ammunition stockpile. She returned to the safehouse.

At the back gate, two MARCOS were stationed, for that was the most vulnerable point from the jungle side.

She had her right hand in the jacket, like always.

They smiled back at her unsuspectedly.

Sasha moved her hands with the pistol in a flash, and even though the MARCOS trusted her, that wasn't a friendly move.

Something was wrong, but a second was lost. They started to raise their guns, but Sasha shot—on point through their eyes—and the long night had started. Sasha had gone rogue.

Sasha hid both bodies, for she needed some more time to summon her comrades. Then she took the lift to the basement and walked to the communication room. She knew the ins and out of the communication room by now. Sasha had tested the lift and rehearsed the sequence many times earlier just for this day. She checked her watch. Thapa would be busy clearing the dinner utensils while the commandos would be in the gear room, changing shifts. She entered the vacant room and wasted no time in resetting the transmitters to send encrypted signals—a signal to her comrades lurking in the vicinity to join her. Sasha had been using the communication room, one of the best Indians had, all this while to coordinate for the Cortex attack. It never surfaced, because it was never tracked. She was hiding in their safe corner and using their own strengths against them.

She sent radio messages at preset low frequencies and waited. After fifteen minutes, she saw movement near the entrance road. They had arrived. Since Abhimanyu had left, the security had been heightened. It was to be tested tonight. Sasha locked the communication room, went straight to the stairs leading to the lobby and waited for the first shot. She heard two shots. And then a flurry of shots. A gunfight had broken out. They had to kill everyone before anyone or any word escaped the bungalow. All possible communication lines had already been cut. Sasha went to the kitchen to find Thapa as her men spread out in the bungalow. But Thapa had left. Two other commandos lay dead in kitchen. Thapa had killed one of her men. Thapa could have only gone to one place: the communication room. Sasha ran back through the hallway.

Still struggling to comprehend how they could have entered so secretively, Thapa scrapped his way toward the communication room. He knew the only way out was to call for reinforcements and hide in here under a complete lockdown till help arrived. The communication room had a steel room underneath and only Thapa knew of it. He just had to find Sasha and hide in it. Thapa reached the communication room. He couldn't understand why it was locked. It was an electronic lock they used, and any attempt to unlock it by force or bullets would only interlock it. It also meant Sasha was not here, and he'll have to find her after calling for reinforcements. This was Thapa's home, and he knew another way to get into the communications room. Thapa went around the back, climbed a tree and jumped through a very narrow ventilation into a duct that led straight to the room.

Sasha scouted for Thapa in the house. While she didn't find him there, she heard the noise of a thud—something falling inside the communication room. She returned to it, opened it and saw Thapa about to enter some codes.

Thapa turned around, saw her with a gun and was relieved to see her alive. He smiled. The last expression on Thapa's face was as much of shock as was of hope. Even in his last moments, Thapa couldn't comprehended Sasha's true identity.

Sasha's team had completely seized the house.

It had been a call from Al Malik himself that prompted Sasha to intervene. Indians had proved to be more than handy, and Aaleyah was activated to service. Sasha kneeled in the communications room and recollected all the vows she had taken. Salvation day had arrived. After more than ten years, she could finally shed her fake identity and embrace her true self.

For her comrades, she was Aaleyah and not just Sasha. Coronated by Al Malik with the title, Aaleyah was akin to a holy figure. They worshipped her; they would die for her. She was the protector of the believers and murderer of the infidels. She served only the realm. Though that was only true in parts, for three men could command her and one had given her an assignment today. Aaleyah finished her prayers and rose. She met everyone in the lobby.

They kneeled.

She signaled them to stand with both hands. 'All clear?'

'Yes,' they responded.

'Rasheesh, are the wheels in place?'

'Yes.'

'It has been taken from the tank and is now on its way to Guwahati. We'll cross it in about fifteen minutes. We can then join the convoy.'

Like Rupesh, Rasheesh was another renegade Indian soldier—the one who had sold his country for the money, another Indian spy who had defected after a handsome payment from Bilal. 'We need to activate it and attach a timer. Once the timer is on, no one can prevent it.'

'Don't forget, the Indians had Khalid and even the hard disk.'

Rasheesh realized she was abreast with the latest situation. 'We've taken care of it. It has been deleted.'

'Wow, how did you manage that?'

'We have friends inside. They don't know what's coming their way, and they were easy to convince for a small fortune.' Rasheesh smirked.

'We still need a hideout.'

'You're right, and I've arranged for the perfect hideout to activate it.'

Aaleyah was tracking. 'Then let's go. Let the Indians figure out what happened here. I'm sure that will take them a good amount of time before they shift gears.'

CHAPTER 22

THE LAST LAUGH

Guwahati Command Center

A large part of the room was jubilant. They had stopped a catastrophe—a global war. It was earned through extreme sacrifice and was well deserved. The celebrations were unlike of men in uniform. It was a mission like no other that he had seen in his career. Arup realized they needed it to release all the tension that had built up in the last few days. The celebrations were in time for the first rays of the morning sun to welcome them to a bright dawn. For once, Arup let his guard down, though he knew a lot of closets would be shaken up to the core now.

Amjad stood in a corner and served himself a glass of Johnnie Walker Blue, top of the line. It was Akram's favorite drink, and Amjad had hoped to share it with him at the end of the mission. Fate had other plans. Amjad decided to raise the first toast of the mission's success to Akram.

The country had staved off a nuclear threat, but the forces were only beginning to count their share of losses. The revelations made in the last few days would reverberate for a long time in the halls of Delhi. The veteran administrator in him knew another storm was coming. The far-reaching implications of a mole that had been in the system for ten years couldn't be quantified. The mole had walked amongst them, had married the best of them, and had become family. Perhaps she had crossed sides, or perhaps she had been an agent since the very beginning. No one knew these details, but these questions needed an answer. Hopefully, they would soon find out. They had her in custody now.

'Sure it is her?' Sonia joined him.

Amjad nodded. 'The face scanner is not human, thankfully. Besides, that was the only face I could see clearly even through that darkness.'

'And she stabbed Abhimanyu, of all people,' Sonia said slowly, almost to herself.

'She has been stabbing Abhimanyu and the rest of us ever since she joined the forces. The one we saw on screen was only one instance.'

The celebratory cheering had moved farther away, and the sun was shining brighter now. The silence amplified the noise of treachery, occasionally interrupted by winds moving down the Himalayas. The rays betrayed their purpose. It was not a new dawn but just another day.

'I have a feeling this has not stopped yet.'

'What do you mean?' Sonia asked, surprised.

Amjad poured himself another glass of the fine scotch whisky and looked at her. 'She tried to flee with the black tab even after the nuke was disabled.'

'Escape attempt?'

'Why go for the black tab then? Why not just fly off?'

Amjad's logic was frightening for a moment, but Sonia decided to give it a break. Maybe it was just the whisky talking. After all, they just had a hell of a few weeks. The paranoid spy in him needed some rest, for there were more pressing issues now. 'I'm more worried about Abhimanyu. His wounds are deep and many. A stab and two shots.'

Amjad nodded. 'I think we'll be lucky if he survives that kind of blow.' And added with some hope, 'But he's a fighter.'

'Mentally?'

Amjad glanced at her and shied away from an answer. In that fleeting look, he was desperate for Sonia to be right. Abhimanyu would need more emotional support even if his body survived miraculously.

'He has been one of the toughest recruits, survived many scars. But this … this is a different ballgame.' Even with Amjad's experience, he had never seen anyone go through such odds.

A soldier approached him. 'Sir, we have a call from Delhi.'

'At this hour?' It was six in the morning. The Babus never arrived so early to the office.

'Sir, the prime minister's on the line.'

'Oh …' Amjad wasn't in the best frame of mind. He realized a call was due anyway. Amjad walked to a corner and inserted his earpiece.

'Sir, are we clear to patch him up?'

'Yes, of course.'

'Amjad, the nation owes you a debt. You and your men have saved all of us once again.'

Amjad was moved by a personal call but not enraptured as one would have imagined. 'Thank you, sir. We've suffered our share of losses this time.'

The prime minister sensed his sober mood.

'I understand. How's your team?'

'Not well, actually. We had a few casualties. Akram is dead. Two more MARCOS are critical. And the guy I had selected, Abhimanyu, has been stabbed and shot.'

'Oh, I see.'

'By his wife,' Amjad added the minor detail.

'Sorry, what do you mean?'

'We've been breached, sir. She was one of us. We understand now that she was a sleeping agent. We've captured her but not before she had stabbed our mission lead who also happened to be her husband.'

After a long pause, the prime minister said, 'Be that as it maybe, we have averted a global war. UN office had been put on a high alert. All of that can be put behind now. I'll await a report from you on the details.'

'Sure, sir. Sir, one more thing. Radha, the IB Deputy Director, was also a mole. Delhi Police will go public with it with a managed paper trail, but his tentacles had deep roots in Cortex.'

'Hmm …' A long silence came from the prime minister's end. 'This has gone too deep for our comfort. Perhaps it comes with the rising profile of our country. The important thing is we have it under control now. I'll wait for your classified report.'

'Sir.'

'Amjad, this will shine on your file.' The prime minister waited for him to acknowledge it, but he was treated with silence. 'I'll be recommending you for the post of NIA Director in the new setup.'

NIA was the new nodal intelligence agency instituted as a central body to run counterterrorism and counterespionage operations. It was a standard political reaction to every major attack in the country – a new nodal agency that would flip the existing hierarchies among the spy agencies. So, like every time, substantial personal lobbying was underway on the red carpets of Janpath. The post had just gone to someone who had been the farthest from all of it.

'Sir.' He acknowledged it without any hint of exultation and only with a dutybound sense of service. Amjad would now have direct access to foreign counterterrorism and counterespionage agencies, all known Indian assets across the globe and a much larger subset of classified information. He won't have to call in others for favors; instead, the others would call him for it. In effect, he would be the second most important man in the Indian security apparatus, only next to the National Security Advisor, Amjad's longtime friend. The only thing to despise was it would also put him at the center of interagency coordination and the politics that came along with it.

There were still a few things Amjad couldn't discuss on the line. 'I'd need to meet you physically, sir,' he said in a burst of spontaneity.

'Sure. My office will connect you soon.' The prime minister didn't inquire much. He knew Amjad well by now. Such requests were typically followed by conversations that could only be spoken about in person.

'Thank you, sir.' The call was done. Amjad kept the phone down. The promotion was a thought bygone. His thoughts returned to Abhimanyu. He called the soldier who had been waiting to be released, standing a few meters away. 'Get me my Jeep.' He turned to Sonia. 'We need to visit the military Hospital.'

The terrorists had been taken to the high security army intelligence hospital situated near the Guwahati military hospital. Situated in the outskirts of Guwahati, it was amply disguised for seekers. A vast stretch of land lay barren deep inside the well-guarded military cantonment. It was a well-disguised helipad capable to accommodate twenty helicopters at a time. At the end of the ground, a stone structure of Scottish baronial vintage rose to the skies—an imprint of the imperial times—and the army had converted it into a hundred-bed hospital since then.

Amjad arrived at the gates. 'Where is he?'

Major Prakash, area commander of the army intelligence unit, showed him through the alley to block M5, room 216 where Abhimanyu was being treated.

'And where is she?' he inquired about Sasha.

'Quarantined underground in the army intelligence wing. Block G1, room 119.'

The underground facility was a specially secluded place rarely opened to visitors. Very few people even knew about its existence. Many layers of security protocol and a ten-ton metallic door separated it from the outside world. To avoid any suspicion on personnel, all the sleuths here were officially on the military hospital's payroll that operated from the front of the compound and catered to only defense families living in the cantonment. The facility had different entrance and exit points to set apart the visitors. Only senior military officers with the right top-level clearances could enter the intelligence wing. The checks and balances had ensured that the facility was neve compromised, at least as far as the Indians knew.

Hindu Kush Mountains, January 25

Abdullah Bahri was an angry man. He paced down the dark alleys of a cavern in the deep mountains of Hindu Kush. The cold winds couldn't breach its hull as Abdullah had poured money to carve out a hot bubble for himself here—a safe spot. The cave walls had been reinforced to withstand a barrage of the Tomahawk missiles— the fulcrum of US Navy. This was Al Malik's den of safety amidst the chaos he had orchestrated. Rather, just one of the many he had across the globe hidden from the public eyes. For all that investment, today, he felt as unsafe as a commoner on the road. The Indians had captured Al Malik's own protégé. While very few knew of it, Al Malik had been responsible for Sasha's upbringing. She was the closest to a daughter he'd had, and he had raised her to be a warrior. Abdullah would speak of her with great pride when he was with the other Lords of the Golden Circle. Putting your own family in the line of fire was never easy. It was a statement of personal sacrifice, the highest offering one could make. The few who mattered knew it and respected Abdullah for it. However, he had never thought sacrifice would become a reality one day.

The culprit had arrived. Abdullah sat in his chair and looked at the camera.

This time, his personal guards brought in Bilal. Paths to this cave couldn't be exposed to even the most trustworthy of his assets. They had picked him up in the nearby town of Chitral and brought him to this cavern in the Wakhan corridor nature reserve at the trijunction of India, Pakistan, and Afghanistan border. Bilal shivered, for he knew he would pay a price for the failure, but he wasn't sure to what extent.

The men boarded him on the wooden lift. 'Stand still.'

The blindfold was tight, but Bilal could tell he was underground. The smell of the rocks and the brush of the hot air was conspicuous. He budged toward the walls.

'Don't move if you want to stay alive.' The guard stopped him.

Bilal felt the gravity churn in his stomach and realized a lift was transporting him somewhere deeper underground. Heat and humidity increased exponentially as their distance from the ground increased. Soon, it became unbearable. The creaking iron shafts of the moving lift made him more nervous. Sweat covered Bilal's face, hands, legs, and even groin. The lift hit the floor with a bang that almost threw Bilal off balance.

The guard caught him.

Bilal was scared now. It felt worse than he had expected. The lift door opened, and Bilal saw a ray of light brighten the blindfold. He remembered the instructions to stand still and obeyed. The light ray was followed by a gush of cold wind, dry and unnatural. It must be a centralized air-conditioning unit, Bilal guessed. A semblance of normality returned to him.

The men took his hands and pulled him from the lift.

'Careful. You're dealing with an officer,' Bilal said.

They ignored him, took him to a large hall where his steps reverberated back to him and finally opened his blindfold.

'Where am I?'

'Only we ask the questions here.' The handlers were wearing masks.

Bilal gauged their specs immediately—military grade, anti-gas. Not many militaries carried them, but he wasn't surprised. After all, these were Abdullah's men.

'Follow us.'

Bilal walked with them. The comforting cold air humidified near surfaces with strange patterns. One by one, he passed many cages of bodies of goats, pigs, mules, camels, leopard, and even a tiger. He realized the animals were being subjected to chemical experiments. Certainly, governments on either side of the border weren't aware of it. The specimens were in a bad condition. Some of them were perhaps even dead. Bilal was shaken, and his confidence was sinking by the moment.

They entered another large hall with marble floor and black stone linings. Their steps reverberated off the shiny surfaces and filled the air with an echo. The acoustics were designed to intimidate.

'Please sit here.'

The echo of the voice startled Bilal. He immediately sat on the chair. At the center of the room, another chair with cushions stood out at an elevated height. These hair-raising mannerisms had spooked him enough, and he just wished to get done with this as soon as possible. A veteran officer himself, Bilal recognized the theatrics. The army officer in him was enraged. He had helped Al Malik raise billions of dollars in Pakistan, Middle East, and Africa. Even though they had failed this time, he expected a better treatment. The cow they had been feeding for so long had lost the sense of gratefulness. In his mind, Bilal decided to make Al Malik pay for this treatment once he had things under his control. Holy as he may be, the line had to be understood, both ways.

He heard footsteps. The sounds reverberated, and it felt like stereo surround sound. No one was visible yet. A lone shadow emerged from the dark corridor behind the heightened chair. It was indeed Abdullah Bahri, whom he was seeing after twenty-five years finally. Bilal bowed his head.

Al Malik took the chair. 'Five years of effort, sweat, and money. Everything went down the drain.'

'We will strike again, Al Malik,' Bilal said, his head still bowed.

'Of course. But first, we need to pay penance for this failure.'

Bilal looked up with fear. 'Yes, Al Malik. As you wish.' Bilal wanted to get out of here alive at any cost. 'You are right. We need to make an example out of it.'

'I am told your recruit from the army, Rup … What's his name?'

'Rupesh, Al Malik.'

'Yes. He spoke.'

Al Malik had his own sources independent of Bilal. The thought scared him more. 'We should have never trusted that Indian. He was just a traitor.' Bilal disbanded Rupesh, or at least pretended to show disdain. In his own mind, he knew Rupesh was the best money could buy.

'How did they get Subramanian's coordinate?'

'ISI is working on it, Al Malik. Our sources in RAW are also working on it.'

'Your sources? Your sources couldn't even protect Aaleyah!' A fit of rage engulfed Abdullah.

Bilal sat with his head down. For twenty-five years, they hadn't met each other in person. Today, they were scheduled to meet and celebrate the success. Instead, it was Bilal's greatest moment of failure.

'I had asked you to take care of her!' Al Malik said in an emotional way Bilal had never heard before.

'I sent more men to protect her.'

'Yes, but incompetent. All of them. Just as you were. They couldn't use the bomb, couldn't keep their mouths shut, and couldn't protect Aaleyah.' Abdullah lost his cool and made some hand gestures.

Bilal looked up, and shadows reappeared behind him; they guards were back. Almost immediately, Bilal's chair heated up. The seats were wet and sticky. He tried to jump, out of reflex, but his clothes were stuck to the chair. He was stuck. It became clear that Al Malik would punish him for his failure. Till a moment ago, Bilal was still contemplating retaliation at Abdullah Bahri for this treatment, but now, he just wanted to survive. 'What are you doing?'

'Just what you said.' Abdullah smiled, and the lights brightened. 'Setting an example. In a war, you win, or you die.'

'I have sacrificed everything for you. I have served you for so long and ever so honestly. Why me?'

'Not as much as Aaliyah.' Al Malik called the guard and handed him his gun.

Bilal wondered what was so special about this Aaleyah; after all, they are meant to be sacrificed one day in the war. Bilal had only heard stories of Abdullah Bahri's punishments. But there was definitely more to this than just revenge. 'No, no! Spare me. I'll get her out. I promise.'

The shot went right through his temples even as he was pleading. The shirt, glued to the chair, prevented his body from tipping over, but his head fell forward and stared at the floor, dead.

'Because no one plays around with my daughter's life.'

CHAPTER 23

THE RIVER

Military Hospital, Guwahati

India would celebrate another Republic Day without a terrorist incident. However, the human price it had paid was high yet again. No one knew how Abhimanyu's body had survived, but everyone knew why his soul had been crushed. His body recovered well, but his mind had been scarred beyond mends. He had been sleeping under the effect of morphine, but the doctors were struggling to balance morphine dosage with intravenous paracetamol dosages. His mind had shunted reality for his body to rest in peace. The truth was hard to digest and even harder to explain to oneself. Destiny had had played a cruel hand.

An hour ago, Abhimanyu had dozed off under the effect of morphine again. It was wearing off again. The heat in his sweat drained him of his last ounce of energy. His body convulsed; he could feel his breath rise, but he could not yet see anything—anything except one image. As soon as he opened his eyes, he saw Qadir's image in front of him. It was his image from the jungles outside the Bagyidaw's, the last time he had seen him in flesh. Abhimanyu screamed at him in anger but couldn't pull out his hand. The nurse had tied it to the clamps.

Another dose of morphine kept him quiet for a couple hours, but upon opening his eyes, he saw the same image again. He could have killed Qadir that day and not only avenged Bhavya's death but perhaps also stopped the events that had transpired at Bagyidaw's. The sweat on Abhimanyu's face heated by the second and seared through his body till the nurse calmed him with another round of intravenous fluids. The next time Abhimanyu opened his eyes, he saw Qadir's image from the jungles in even more detail. Qadir was looking for him with his fingers on the trigger, ready to shoot. It was all about his failure that night—the mistake that had cost him the lives of Akram, Siddhartha, Thapa, and many other commandos.

Abhimanyu searched for an escape, but the walls were closing in on him even as, still by still, his portray in the vignette disappeared. But another image appeared, that of Sasha this time. His mind relapsed, and his soul froze for a moment. He felt love and hate simultaneously. He felt a surging heat inside him again, only to be interrupted by an occasional beep that dialed down gradually, but a louder siren simultaneously took over—an emergency call for the doctor.

Even as the nurse increased the paracetamol dosage, she was failing to control the temperature.

'Give me the defibrillator.'

The nurse handed it to the doctor. 'Why is he shouting?' the nurse asked worryingly.

'He's hallucinating.' The doctor knew he didn't have much time. Abhimanyu was going through a bad dream, and the mental trauma was paralyzing Abhimanyu's body. They had to break the chain. 'His temperature is one hundred and six.' It would be a miracle if he recovered from here without any brain damage. Abhimanyu's body was self-inflicting irreparable damage. The doctor used the defibrillators and prevented him from going into a coma.

His heartbeat regularized, and they put him on heavy fluids to lower the temperature. He had survived by a whisker. Death was still knocking at his doors.

'We need continuous monitoring on all the vitals,' the doctor announced and left a nurse stationed permanently.

Meanwhile, Amjad had spotted the slayer. He looked through the glass window of room 119 just wide enough to sneak a peek. She had regained consciousness and was as calm as the sea, unperturbed by her surroundings—no fear, no remorse, and no sign of anxiety. It was a trained blank expression. Amjad recognized it when he saw one. She stood to have a glass of water and went back to sleep. Amjad realized she was mentally preparing for the interrogations ahead, the ways of which she knew all too well. Her demeanor and cool, calm confidence oozed years of practice and rigorous training. She was much more than what appeared on the surface and wouldn't be easy to break.

'Can she talk?' he asked Major Prakash who had just entered and stood beside him.

'Medically, she is more than fit to talk. Nothing stops her from talking, but she hasn't spoken a word to anyone yet. No action, no reaction, not even a gesture. The only thing she cares is to take her medicines as prescribed, drink water, and eat timely.'

'Following the manual.' Amjad deduced she was conserving her energy and recovering. With every observation, his estimation of her training only increased.

'Heard she is a spy. She was on the inside?' Prakash eyed Amjad.

He nodded. 'Which makes her very dangerous. I want you to have twenty-four-hour surveillance on her. Your men should shadow her everywhere she goes, including the washroom.'

Prakash nodded uncomfortably. 'We'll get women for that.' He smiled awkwardly.

'Construct an online observation room and get cameras inside her room as well. Do whatever you need to keep her under constant watch.'

'Sir, she can't pull a smart one here.' Major Prakash had taken offence to Amjad's thought; this place was impenetrable.

'That doesn't prevent her from trying.' Prakash was still not fully onboard, but Amjad couldn't tell him about Cortex, for it was still classified. 'See, I trust your protocols, but we just can't be careful enough on this one. Remember Decot?'

Major Prakash's face yellowed. He remembered Decot too well—the attack that had almost blew Chennai to ashes. 'What about Decot?'

'Something similar has happened again. Only this time, they came even closer.'

'We'll do just as you say, sir.' The mere mention of Decot was enough.

Details of the shootout in the Siang hills would be under wraps for a long time. Intelligence agencies were sanitizing the village, but he knew a leak was eventually inevitable. Amjad had his one eye on the cleanup underway. They'd have to get their public story right by the time it was finished. No story could explain Sasha's acts without embarrassment. No spin would conceal a human breach of such magnitude. What would happen to their credibility? And with such low credibility, how could they guarantee no such breach would happen ever again? That was as far as the public management was concerned. Internally, he had even bigger problems to tackle. The real cost to the agency's operations due to this breach would unfold with time. Segregating friends from foe across the entire intelligence apparatus was incomprehensible. They would have to vet every asset and employee. It was an impractical exercise but necessary. There was only one way to short circuit this laborious task.

'I need her across the table as soon as she is ready.'

'In an hour, sir?'

'No sooner?' Amjad was longing.

'We're waiting for her morning reports—blood, urine, stool, liver, kidney, swab, and X-rays. The entire roll,' Prakash responded.

'You've missed the most important one. Get me the polygraph machine.'

Polygraph Room, Military Cantonment, Guwahati

They sat quietly across the table. Neither was in rush. The others carefully observed them and stood in silence across the glass partition. Custom lights lined the room, but Amjad had chosen to keep it simple today. It was all white. The play of lights was meant to disorient the prisoner, but today, he needed to see her reactions clearly to convince himself.

Major Prakash watched through the tinted glass—an age-old setup for monitoring interrogations—but this glass was different. It could instantly judge a person's response and predict the probability of truth in their admissions, all of this without the prisoner having the slightest idea that he or she was under observation. The software could also foretell questions to maintain a fruitful line of interrogation. The questions were fed directly to the tab, the one Amjad was staring at now.

'Tell me your name.'

'You know it.'

'Your real name.'

'Sasha Rathore. Always been my real name.'

'You were an Indian Intelligence Officer suspended for incompetence.' He tried to rattle her.

She gave no reaction.

'We caught you with the terrorists responsible for executing Cortex.' He waited to see her response; there was none. 'Can you explain how you ended up with them?'

She stayed quiet.

'Do you know anything about Cortex?'

'I don't know.'

Amjad realized Sasha wouldn't relinquish without a fight, as expected. 'You were caught with them. Fighting for them.'

'I was forced to.' She stared into his eyes with a resolve that wasn't indicative of her captivity.

'What do you mean?'

'You killed my parents when I was five years old. All they had done was heal people, heal your people.'

'No, we didn't.'

'Yes, you did. When you attacked Colombo. My parents were just doctors treating soldiers of both the Sri Lankan Army and the Tamil militias. Both sides respected them for their services until the night the Indians came in.'

Amjad eyed her with intrigue. Was this a new spin? He wasn't sure of the line between the truth and the lie. It was very difficult. He hadn't picked up a single physical cue yet. She was very well trained. He looked at his pad; it was green. She was saying the truth, if the machine could be trusted.

Major Prakash watched Sonia search through databases to corroborate Sasha's story.

Amjad stayed quiet and let her speak.

'The fight between the Tamil Tigers and the Sri Lankan Government was straightforward. Sides were clearly defined, and humanitarian workers, like my parents, just did their job. Both parties gave us the space to operate.' A teardrop fell down her cheek. 'Until that fateful day of December twentieth, 1990. Your commandos came into our lands and attacked the LTTE, killing more than five hundred people overnight. In retaliation, they killed whoever they suspected to provide the Indians with any support. There were no lines any longer. There was only one right side for both sides.'

'Why do you blame the Indians?'

She stayed quiet.

'It was a fight between the Sri Lankans and the Tamil militias. How did we kill them?'

'Exactly. You had no business to interfere. My parents died at the hands of Indian forces trying to run away from the Tamil militias. They were killed for being good citizens of their land.'

Her story matched the records. Sonia located a certain Dr. Illembiar Kottaka and Dr. Irena Kottaka killed in the crossfire. The Indian forces attributed it to the Tamil militias, and the Tamil militias attributed it to the Indian forces. The Kottakas were covered extensively in newspapers for their philanthropic activities. Sonia found the many references quite easily. They had two kids. Sasikala Kottaka and Rumilia Kottaka. On that fateful night, both their kids were also reported to have been killed—or not really. Sonia studied Sasha again and ran a face match from one of the newspaper photos. It was Rumilia indeed. She had grown up to be Sasha.

Amjad checked the pad; it was green. Surprised, he asked her the next logical question. 'Who recruited you?'

'No one. I recruited myself.'

This time, the tab was red.

'So tell me, who were you supposed to meet after the mission?'

'God.' She smiled. 'We were meant to die with the mission.'

'But you were trying to escape.'

Sasha looked the other way. 'I had a change of mind. We didn't have a backup plan until you got there.' It was a lie again.

Amjad caught her blinking a little slower every time she lied. 'I know you had to meet someone.'

Sasha regarded him, stone-faced. 'I have my own birds.'

Amjad knew she was judging him, but she reveal any leads.

'No one, I said. Good luck with your birds. But yes, we were fed our backup plans well in advance.' She had flipped.

Amjad noticed she had blinked slower this time. She couldn't be lying both ways. The machine had lost it completely by now, and Amjad was more comfortable without it. Sasha was playing with him. She was trained to be a bland listener and a proficient liar. Amjad saw through it in amazement but realized the one constant in her flips. She was protecting her handler. 'That's it for today.' He ended it abruptly, which surprised her. Amjad left the room and looked through the glass panels. 'She is good. We need to find a way to break her.'

'What if we get Abhimanyu in there?'

Amjad glared at Major Prakash for suggesting it. On second thought, he repeated that line to himself.

'They were married after all, and there could be emotional chinks. We can exploit it,' Prakash insisted to both Sonia's and Amjad's displeasure.

Even if Amjad accepted it, Sasha was on her feet, but Abhimanyu wasn't ready. It might be an option, if and when he heals completely.

Sasha was still an unknown entity. How did she get out of Sri Lanka? Who was her guardian after her parents died? How did she become a spy for Pakistan? Who were her helpers in India? Amjad needed answers to many more questions before he could get ahold of her thought process. From what he had seen, she would break Abhimanyu emotionally, unless Abhimanyu was fully ready and back in his elements. Exposing Abhimanyu to her before that was not even an option.

Amjad ignored the request for now but notated it.

Prakash took Amjad to another room nearby and left them alone. Sasha's room was down the same corridor, and Prakash went to inspect it.

'Why don't you check the control room? See if everything is okay there,' Amjad asked Sonia, and she promptly left him. Amjad had to catch up with the aftermath in Delhi. He dialed in Shankar Menon, the national security advisor. 'Did you get my message?'

'Yes, shocking. We were looking in the mountains, and it sat amongst us all this while.' After some thought, Shankar continued, 'Amjad, you and your team have been through a lot. Why don't you take a leave for some time?'

As much as Amjad agreed with the first part, he couldn't leave amidst such crisis. 'You know I can't. I dialed you to get some extra resources.'

Shankar hadn't expected any other response. Even though Shankar wished him a break, he was happy to have him around in the politically uncertain times to come and was more than happy to help. 'Always on job. What do you need?'

'I need to know everyone Sasha had spoken to, met, or interacted with in the entire time she was in India. For that, I'll require people who are good at disguising themselves.'

Shankar realized they had to be from outside the system. 'How many?'

'Around a dozen guys. We need to finish this as soon as possible, say, in a week.'

It was a tall ask, but Shankar needed to close all the loose ends before anything leaked to the media or the public, which was only a matter of time. 'My office will get you a list of civilians working for us along with all the security clearances. It shouldn't take more than a couple hours.'

'Thanks, Shankar. I'll see you soon.'

'Amjad?'

'Sir.'

'Are you okay?'

It was an unfair question. So was life. Unfair. Amjad centered himself quickly, for it was a genuine question out of concern. 'We have to live with it, Shankar. Like most other things in life.'

Shankar acknowledged the hardships, and they signed off. Amjad closed his eyes but couldn't stop himself from imagining the magnitude of the breaches. He recognized his behavior was bordering paranoia. Shankar was right; he desperately needed a break.

The sun was blinding, but he went to the window to get some fresh air. The expansive security apparatus at the military hospital was moving through its motions like a well-oiled machine. The massive manpower and advanced technology deployed came in sync with each other fluidly. All the security, setup, and technology was still no match for a simple human breach. Amjad had learnt it the hard way. Just one person in the right place at the right time could compromise the place. *I need the identities of all the men working at this hospital*, he messaged Prakash.

Amjad watched a grocery truck enter through the checkpoint, followed by another army convoy which was checked thoroughly with dogs and sensors despite it being their own. Next was the commanding officer's Jeep; no exceptions were made either. The security was comprehensive. An ambulance entered with a few patients. Another refrigerated truck for the deceased followed. Amjad noticed the logo on the ambulance also adorned the refrigerated truck. It wasn't army's. The dogs checked the vehicles.

Major Prakash interrupted his thoughts. 'Abhimanyu is awake.'

'Can we talk to him?'

'Yes. His body is responding well to the medicine now.'

Amjad nodded; he had another query to clear. 'Tell me, since when did we allow civilian trucks inside the military hospital?'

Prakash looked through the window and recognized the logo. 'Oh, that is just complying with the new rules of bureaucracy. Outsourcing is the mantra. We have outsourced our medical supplies to third-party vendors. Saves a ton of cost. Some babu in the defense ministry gets finance ministry off his back, and some other babu in finance ministry gets his KRA ticked.' He looked at Amjad. 'Don't worry. These are empaneled vendors. We do a thorough background check.'

'Of course.' He had heard that many times before. The truck cleared the three security gates one by one as Amjad recalled Abhimanyu. 'Have you also outsourced anything in the army intelligence wing?'

'Not a chance. Too sensitive.' The bureaucracy had creeped in far too deep into the military.

Amjad was setting up his priorities as the NIA Director already. Finance ministry couldn't decide on security matters. It had to stop.

*****

Abhimanyu was awake. They slowly opened the door and walked to his bedside.

The nurse checking his vitals left the room as they entered.

'Doctor says you're recovering well,' Amjad said, breaking the ice.

Abhimanyu smiled and looked toward the window.

Leaving the two to themselves, Major Prakash swiped his fingers on the scanner in the door and left.

'Every room has a scanner. Lot of security in here.' Amjad tried some small talk despite knowing he wasn't good at it.

'Can you believe it?'

'I really can't.'

'I couldn't see through her at all.'

'To be fair, none of us did.' Amjad tried to lighten his load.

'I married her, slept with her, dreamt of a family with her, and was even planning to retire for her.'

'It's not your fault. Don't be too hard on yourself. We never doubt the people closest to us. It was the system's failure. It should have recognized her traces long ago.'

Abhimanyu gave no reaction. He did not need sympathy.

'Well, at least the silver lining is you won't retire now.'

Abhimanyu finally grinned. 'Yes, that's definitely out the window now.' He spied the kettle.

Amjad poured him some water.

'Do we have her?'

Amjad nodded.

'Do we have anything on her yet?'

'Did you know her upbringing was in Sri Lanka?' Amjad quietly settled in his chair.

'No. I thought she was an Indian. Anything else?'

'I'm afraid, not yet. She is good.'

Abhimanyu couldn't wait to sit across the table and quiz her. The game had changed colors, and he wanted revenge now. 'She is well trained?'

'Yes. One of the best.'

Abhimanyu smirked.

The lights flickered a few times and eventually went out. After a couple moments, the backup power lit the room.

'That's weird.' Amjad looked around. It was eerie in an army facility.

'What's next for you?'

'NIA.'

The lights flickered and tripped again. This time, it took longer for it to come back.

'Something is wrong.' Amjad stood, and his phone rang; it was Major Prakash. 'Why are the lights flickering?'

'We're under attack. Gunmen, perhaps fedayeen.' He had never heard a soldier's voice so frightened. 'They've breached the gates and are inside the army intelligence hospital wing.''Where is the firing happening?'

'G1 block.'

Amjad frowned. 'Sasha. They're here for her.'

'You have to go,' Abhimanyu said.

'I can't leave you behind.' Amjad would not take chances.

A thunderous knock sounded at their door. Two masked gunmen looked through the door window.

Amjad looked back at them and unholstered his pistol.

The gunmen shot at the door, but the room was bulletproof. Each door, made of a ton of steel, could only be opened with due authorizations.

Amjad shouted into the phone almost in a panic, which was very unlike of him, 'They are into the military wing as well!'

The gunmen shot at the glass, but it held up.

'My men are on their way. Don't open the door. Stay there,' Prakash said, but Amjad wasn't sure how long the glass would hold.

Amjad realized he couldn't stay there for long either. He had to be out there, fighting the fedayeens.

'You have to go, Amjad.'

He nodded. 'And you will come with me,' he said to Abhimanyu, gently removing all the intravenous connectors then helping him get onto the window. Amjad knew the safest place for Abhimanyu. There could be no safer place than the underground bunker now, and every floor had access to it. He helped Abhimanyu through the window railings and followed him through.

Thanks to the shadows between the buildings, no one had a direct sight of them. Once they reached the corridor, Amjad kneeled forward to check. Two men lay dead—medical staff. There was no other noise. Amjad helped Abhimanyu to the lift at the end of the corridor. The lift would take him to the underground bunker directly. 'Stay there. Don't come out.' He gave him his Glock 26.

'What about you?'

'I'll manage.' He pressed the lift button.

Abhimanyu was secured.

Amjad turned back and took the stairs. After crossing two levels, he heard shots. The terrorists were approaching the fire exit. They couldn't access the lifts, so they were using staircases to move from one floor to another. They were coming to him. Amjad hid behind the wall and waited for them. He heard two distinct footsteps. As the boots neared, Amjad took a deep breath and stopped breathing.

The first of them opened the door and moved forward. He was laced with grenades, ready to sacrifice his life.

Amjad let the second gunman behind him enter the corridor. He was in a dark spot behind the door—a blind spot to the fedayeens. As soon as the second gunman entered, Amjad emerged with his hands first and pounced on his wrists. After a three-finger press, he directed the gun at the first gunman who was right ahead and shot him in the head before he could turn back. Amjad hit the second gunmen at his knee, and, as he fell to the wall, he shot him in the head. Amjad grabbed their semi-automatic and left.

He rushed from wall to wall and entered the army intelligence wing. He swiped his card and went straight for the control room to Major Prakash. Amjad planned to take a contingent and secure Sasha. Amidst sporadic gunshots, Amjad strode from one alley to another, which were completely empty. Everyone had locked themselves inside the steeled rooms. Finally, he reached the control room. After a credential check, the door opened.

'Are you okay?' Major Prakash asked.

'Barely. How many of them are there?'

'Twelve. We've launched two assault teams. Four of the terrorists have been neutralized.'

'Why have they come here to die?'

'I don't know. They seem to be withdrawing. They've formed a cordon and are pushing toward the parking area. If they have an exit plan from there, our snipers will take them out as soon as they emerge.'

'And what about Sasha?'

'Safe and secured. Still inside her room, locked down.' He put her on the screen.

She lay on her bed calmly and seemingly unperturbed by the shooting.

Amjad didn't like the smell of it. 'They didn't come in here to die then only try to escape now?'

'I don't know why they've come in here. But they've surely chosen a wrong target.' Prakash's confidence was in stark difference to Amjad's paranoia.

'Sir, firing at the officer's mess.'

The sharp voice disturbed Prakash greatly. His confidence vanished in thin air, and a pale expression crossed his face. At least fifteen unarmed officers were inside the officer's mess. Without wasting any time, Prakash grabbed his transceiver. 'Team Alpha and Team Charlie, move to the officer's mess, secure the mess. I repeat, secure the mess. Unarmed officers under attack.

I repeat, unarmed officer's under attack.' If they were to die unarmed, it would be an unforgivable disaster.

All eyes were on the mess now. Amjad watched attentively. Things were moving too fast. He looked at the screen with Sasha.

She was still on it, lying down with the calmness of a monk. She stood to have a glass of water.

Amjad studied the screen, trying to see the time on the clock in the background. Everything became as clear as the sky to him. 'Prakash, get your men right down in G1 block now! The video feed is doctored!'

Panic struck the control room.

'What do you mean doctored?'

'Look at the time. It says ten a.m. It is an old feed.'

They had been played. Prakash was shellshocked and stood there motionless.

Amjad shook him. 'Send in a team, Prakash. Now.'

Prakash regained his consciousness and to the transceiver. 'Team Charlie, come in! Team Charlie, come in! Move in to secure G1 block, immediately! Get me the real feed, now,' Prakash demanded as his men scurried to ascertain the problem.

Sonia inspected the panels. 'Sir, it is not an encryption. Someone is there. He's physically severed the feed. The network feed from G1 is unavailable.' Sonia was appalled.

'This is the worst day of my life.' Prakash had been completely outwitted.

A blast ripped through the army intelligence wing. The walls held, but the waves shattered anything else that came its way. Prakash could feel the vibrations even in the control room secured with tons of steel shield. Abhimanyu's bunker was shaken to its core.

A large dust bowl rose through the rubble over the army intelligence wing parking bay and rendered the snipers useless. Video feed from Sasha's room had gone blank. The security analyst shifted to another live camera barely functioning. It had a view of her room from the alley.

The pictures were hazy but told a grisly story. The blast had destroyed everything in the vicinity with no trace of life. Time had stopped ticking for Amjad. After several minutes, Team Charlie reached the spot only to find her bed shredded to pieces. There was no evidence of any life lost there—no body pieces, no muscles, or blood spatter. She was not dead.

The firing at the officer's mess had also stopped with the blast, as if the dust bowl had devoured the gunmen. But Amjad couldn't find any fedayeen bodies near the mess either. It was time to accept the reality.

'We've lost her,' Amjad announced, overlooking Prakash, who sat in the control room with his head in his folded hands, drowning in his own failure.